The
Sky
at
Our
Feet

ALSO BY
NADIA HASHIMI

One Half from the East

NADIA HASHIMI

The Sky at Our Feet

WITHDRAWN

HARPER
An Imprint of HarperCollins*Publishers*

For Mom and Dad—
for giving me the sky

Library of Congress Control Number: 2017942899

ISBN 978-0-06-242193-7

Typography by Erin Fitzsimmons

18 19 20 21 22   CG/LSCH   10 9 8 7 6 5 4 3 2 1

First Edition

*Bring the sky beneath your feet and listen
to Celestial Music everywhere.*
—Rumi

*The sky where we live is no place
to lose your wings so love, love, love.*
—Hafiz

One

Pigeons, no matter what country they live in, share a few important traits. They are smart birds that can learn aerial tricks and navigate their way back home. They will eat just about anything. Carrots, lettuce, bell peppers, rice, and crumbled-up bread. They're not very picky. They do need grit to digest their food, though. That could be little pieces of gravel or ground-up oyster shells if you happen to have oyster shells around.

I do not. There aren't many oysters in this overcrowded city in New Jersey. I can't imagine that there are many oyster shells in Afghanistan either, since the country doesn't touch the ocean.

But there's plenty of gravel around thanks to the

crumbling cement of the chimney and building trim, so the birds on our roof are doing okay. I put out fresh bowls of water for them. I change the water every couple of days. Sometimes the rain does the work for me.

I look up. An airplane has left a thin trail of white cotton behind it. Since I was little, my mother has tested me with riddles she learned as a child in Afghanistan. Each one is a mystery, and I like the challenge of unlocking them. I close my eyes and remember one of them.

What searches the skies without ever leaving its home?

I figured out the answer to that one quicker than she expected.

An eye, I remember saying.

I'm not really supposed to be up here on the roof. My mother wouldn't be too happy if she knew I came up here almost every day to try to train pigeons. Our building is old, and the roof sags in some parts. There isn't any kind of railing either, so I have to be sure I stay clear of the edges. But it's safe if you know what you're doing, and I've been doing this for about a year, after my mom told me about what some of her neighbors used to do back in Afghanistan, long before she moved to New Jersey.

"Leave him alone," I mutter. Of the nine pigeons that live on our roof, Billy is the worst. He's always shoving his way to the food as if he's got more right to it than anyone else. There's nothing that special about him, but he seems to think there is. There's one that's more tan than gray. He (or she) might be older than the others. He's got a scar on one side of his face and doesn't move as fast. The others are pretty timid. It took a long time for them not to fly off the rooftop as soon as I opened the hatch to climb up here. Now they gather around because they know I'll bring something good for them.

They fly off but always come back. I haven't gotten them to do any tricks like the pigeon trainers in Afghanistan have done, but I'm working on it. My mom told me her neighbor back home had pigeons who could do full loops or fly with their bellies up. They would fly miles away to deliver secret messages tied to their feet but still come back home. My pigeons are nowhere close to doing any of that, but if lots of other Afghans have been able to do it, I think there's got to be a way.

I'm about to toss out chunks of buttered bread when a voice catches me off guard.

"What are you doing here?"

I drop the plastic bag I'm holding and spin around. Ms. Raz, our landlord and first-floor neighbor, has poked her head out of the hatch.

"I was just—"

But Ms. Raz is not your average silver-haired woman. She doesn't knit or watch game shows or moan about her aching back. I never see or hear her coming, and yet there she always is, suspicious and cranky.

"Get off the roof this minute! You're not supposed to be up here."

Neither is she, really, unless she wants to have her other hip replaced.

"Sorry," I mumble, trying to hide the bowl of water and rice from Ms. Raz's squinty glare.

Ms. Raz is waiting for me when I climb down the ladder and go back into the building. She follows me as I walk, shoulders slumped, to our third-floor apartment. Each floor is one apartment with windows overlooking the street or the grocery store parking lot behind us. The roof is the only place that gives a view of Elkton. I can see the roof of my school to the east and the train station to the south. I see the road that leads to the laundromat and the park where I broke my arm on the monkey bars.

My mother is inside our top-floor apartment, about to be sorely disappointed by what I've just been caught doing.

"Ms. Raz," I say, trying to find a way out of this. It's October and winter is only a couple of months away. Maybe I could offer to shovel the snow off the sidewalk and steps again.

"Not a chance. Open that door so I can tell your mother where I found you." Ms. Raz's glasses hang on a thin chain around her neck. She's looking at me, waiting for my move. The floorboards creak as I shift my weight and stall.

"Shah-jan, is that you?" my mother's voice calls out from inside the apartment. "Come so we can cut this beautiful cake!"

The cake. This gives me an idea. It'll only work if there's a warm heart somewhere inside Ms. Raz's chest.

"She's been waiting for me," I explain. "It's her birthday today, and I saved some money and bought her a chocolate cake. Would you like a slice?"

Ms. Raz folds her arms across her chest and huffs something about bringing her plants in from the balcony.

"If I ever catch you up there again, I'll have you out of this building in a heartbeat!"

I nod my head solemnly and wait for Ms. Raz to disappear before I open the door. I don't want my mother to spot her standing behind me and figure out I took a detour on my way to pick up the mail.

"*Salaam*, Madar!" I call out. My mother is in the small kitchen with her back turned toward me. I can see her light-blue jeans, her ponytail frizzy from the humidity of the laundromat where she works. The evening news plays in the background. My mom always has the news on, as if there's something she's waiting to hear.

I never really learned much Dari from my mother, but

she does insist that I greet her as all Afghans do, so I say *salaam*, which means peace.

"*Salaam, jan-em!*" she sings. She spins to face me, and I see a plate of seasoned drumsticks and stewed potatoes on our little kitchen table. There's the tiny cake I bought too, with one skinny candle sticking out of it. "I make your favorite foods!"

My mom always wants to practice her English with me, so all our conversations are in English. It's my job to correct her pronunciation and grammar, though she's not always happy when I do it.

"It's your birthday, though, so you should have *made* your favorite foods," I correct her without thinking. The cake is actually a cupcake, but it's all I could afford. It's covered with sprinkles and it takes a lot of self-control not to dip my finger into it for a taste. I'm grateful this moment hasn't been ruined by Ms. Raz.

"How was your school today?" she says, ignoring my correction. She kisses the top of my head and points me to the sink so I can wash my hands.

"Fine," I say. I turn the handle and water sputters out. I give the handle an extra twist and it comes off in my hand. It's an old building, so something's always cracking, leaking, shaking, or breaking. My mom and I have become pretty good at fixing most of it ourselves so we don't have to bother Ms. Raz too often. I open the cabinet under the sink and turn off the water valve so the water won't spray everywhere. Then I reach into our tool drawer and pull a wrench from the pile of dollar-store tools. I twist the tip of the faucet off and find a mesh piece inside. I scrub off some gunk and put the pieces back together. "How was work?"

My mother is standing in front of the television, listening to the news anchor. He's talking about a rally against people who are in this country illegally. I see a picture of people shouting and waving signs around. The signs say things like *America for Americans* and *Go Home*.

I slip the small rubber ring off the inside of the handle. It's torn and there's no way to fix it. I dig into the tool drawer again and find a rubber band. I wrap it around the inside of the handle twice and slide it into place. I put the pieces back together and re-open the valve beneath the sink.

"Ha!" I say, happy to see the rubber band did the trick.

"Dear God," my mother says in Dari.

"What's the matter, Mom?" I say, drying my hands on a rag. I follow her gaze to the television screen and see the angry protest, the things they're saying about people who snuck into the country. "They're just mad at people who broke the rules. You get just as mad when I break rules. Remember what you did when I watched an extra half hour of television last Tuesday?"

I laugh at my own joke.

My mother does not.

"Mom, are you okay?"

She looks like she might cry. She also looks like there's something she wants to tell me. As a matter of fact, she's looked that way for the past few weeks. I suppose I've been waiting for this moment, though I didn't know exactly what I was waiting for.

"Shah-jan," she says slowly. "Me and them—we are the same."

What can she possibly mean by that? She's got nothing in common with those people. My mother doesn't speak Spanish. She didn't sneak into this country in the middle of the night. She speaks English and works a regular job.

"Sit down. It is time I tell you my story."

Suddenly my stomach is on edge. I am nervous. I've asked my mom a million times to tell me stories about Afghanistan. Sometimes she describes a place that sounds like heaven.

The fruits taste like they've been sprinkled with sugar. People open their homes even to strangers so travelers are always fed and cared for. The mountains are tall and proud, more impressive than any skyscraper. Every home has a poet and every home has a musician because words and music give Afghans life. Afghanistan is home to the best horsemen—they can defy gravity on the back of a stallion.

8

For honor and family, an Afghan will go to the ends of the earth. Celebrations are rich and festive—a time for new clothes and money handed to smiling children.

Other times, she winces and just changes the subject. I think that's when she's remembering the not-so-great stuff about Afghanistan. I have a feeling she's going to tell me about that stuff now, and I don't know if I want to hear it.

I sit down at the table. My mother joins me.

"Some things I never told you. But maybe I tell you now why I cannot go back. When I see this," she says, pointing to the angry faces on the television screen, "I don't know what is possible to happen." She leaves the television on. My eyes float between looking at my mother and looking at the protestors.

I don't know how, but I have a feeling that, unlike our leaking faucet, the problem my mother's about to reveal has no quick fix.

Two

My mother puts her elbows on the table.

"Shah-jan, there's something you need to know," she says, her accent becoming heavier. She and Auntie Seema are the only people in the world who call me Shah. It was my father's name, and it means king.

I wish my father were here now for whatever it is my mother is about to tell me.

It's strange to miss someone I've never met, but I do. I've grown up with only a handful of photographs, and most of them are grainy and distant. In one, he's sitting on a sofa, his hair thick and wavy. Mom's head leans on his shoulder, and he has his arm wrapped around her. He's looking at her instead of the camera. This makes me think my father was loving.

In another, he's sitting on a bench next to another man. The man's laughing so hard, his eyes are just slivers. This makes me think my father was funny.

I often stare at the picture of my father on my nightstand. In the picture, he wears a gray dress shirt and jeans. He has his arms folded across his chest and a pen tucked above his ear. He is standing on a mountain road with his back to the steep drop behind him. This makes me think my father was brave.

"What is it, Mom?"

She takes a deep breath.

"I start in the beginning," she decides. "Your father was a journalist in Afghanistan. This I told you. But it was difficult for him to make enough money to pay for rent and support his family. One day, a friend told us about another job. He told us the American soldiers were looking for people to translate for them. Your father was speaking English very good—much better than me."

I imagine my father standing side by side with American soldiers. Did he wear a camouflage uniform? Did he ride in tanks? I've pictured my father a million times but never like this. These are new images floating through my head. My mom takes a deep breath and continues her story.

"He did this work for two years. He was with the soldiers always, and it was dangerous. I did not see him for one month or two months sometimes. I was scared for him. We were married only one year before he start this work. I tell him it is very dangerous but he told me we will have a chance in the future to go to United States and study there. He said the future is more important than anything. One day, there was fighting and he was hurt. We were lucky, though, that it was only his hand. The doctors did surgery to take out some metal and he was better, and we got very good news. The embassy said they will give me a student visa to come here. Your father was very happy for me. He said he will do one more job with the Americans and then apply for the special visa. He was helping them and then they will help him—like friends. I was in this country one month when I find out you are coming. I called your father and he was so happy with this good news."

My mother looks over at my father's picture then drops her gaze back to the table.

"He loved you from the moment I told him. He talked about you like he had been dreaming about you for all his life. He promised to teach you to play soccer and to feed you kebab and rice and help you with your algebra so you will get good grades. He was going to show you off to his friends and take you to the university where he was teaching. He wanted to carry you on his shoulders so the world will be at your feet."

I feel a lump grow in my throat when she says all of this. I think of the time my mother took me to the park with a soccer ball under her arm. We'd passed the ball back and forth, nothing all that serious. She managed to kick the ball straight through my legs but slid on the wet grass and ended up on her backside. We both laughed so hard, but then her laughter turned into crying. I didn't know why then. I think I get it now.

"He was excited to be a father—your father—but he was worried too. He wanted to give his perfect baby a perfect world."

My father hated that bad people were in control of some parts of the country. He hated that money and drugs seemed to be more important than people living freely. He hated that there were women and children begging in the street while criminals drove around in fancy cars. He hated that men who had done really bad things could go on living their lives without even an apology when the people they'd hurt never stopped hurting.

"He loved to be a journalist. He wanted to write the truth about what was happening in Afghanistan. A house of lies was no place to raise a child. That's what he said."

My stomach balls up nervously when my mother tells me this even though everything she's talking about has already happened.

"When his hand was better, it was time for the last job. He liked working with the Americans. He said they left their families so far away to come and fight for the people of Afghanistan. I begged him to be careful. Many people did not like that he was working with Americans. They called him a spy, a traitor. They said terrible things. But he was so stubborn, your father. I remember what he told me. 'A father must give his child the best world and food to eat. How can I ask this child to call me Father if I do not do what a father should?'"

I have started to guess where this story is going, and I want her to stop talking. I like what I've believed until now. I don't want anything to change.

I could shout at my mother and tell her to stop, but then there's the part of me that needs to know how much has been hidden from me. I have my elbows on my knees and my head hangs low. I cannot look at her face. I don't want to see her misty eyes. I think of the picture with my father's arm wrapped around my mother as she leans into him. She looks like she could use someone to lean on right now.

It gets worse.

"He was waiting for the visa. There were some bad people in Afghanistan saying terrible things about your father. The Americans told him don't worry. They said soon he will have the visa. Your father, he promised me everything will be okay and we will be together soon. The people who called him a spy . . ." She pauses to take a deep breath. "One day they showed him he was wrong."

I feel pretty sick to my stomach—almost like I don't know who I am anymore. It's the first time I have felt real fear—the kind that plants a flag in your brain and decides it's going to stay.

The birthday cupcake sits between us, the candle melted down to a waxy puddle. It looks sickening to me now, so unappealing that I wonder if I'm going to empty the contents of my stomach right here in the kitchen.

"It wasn't a car accident," I say to confirm that the story I've always believed about my father's death is not true.

She shakes her head. She brushes her hair from her face and steadies her voice to tell me the rest.

"Family back home called me. I was broken. I want to go there that day but they told me no. They said it wasn't safe for me to come back. The family was getting phone calls, terrible phone calls. Terrible words painted on our door. So I stayed. The police did not find the people who did this. I don't know if they really tried."

Tears stream down my face. I know all this happened to my mom a long time ago, but it feels like it's all happening to me, for the first time, right now.

"It seemed crazy that I have to still read my books like nothing happened," she says, folding and unfolding a sheet of paper towel. I can see how her dreams of becoming a doctor fell apart.

My mother stuck with her classes, trying not to break down in biology and doing her best to keep the numbers straight in calculus. My father used to send her some money for clothes, food, and books. She worked part time in a laboratory on campus to support herself too, but she had a hard time doing that when she lost him.

"I wondered if all the crying I did hurt you. I wonder if that's why you are born too soon."

I know the rest of the story. I came early, days before the start of the new year. Instead of being born after nine months, I was born after six. Sidewalks were glazed with ice. People's words hung like thought clouds in the cold air. My mother spent two months at my side in the hospital, watching me grow in a warmed incubator instead of in her belly.

You must give him a name, they told her. She told them the name she and my father had chosen for me.

Sardar Shah.

The nurses tried to say the name. It sounded awful to my mother and she wondered if that was how all Americans would say it.

"There was one nurse. She was good to me," my mother had explained. "She helped me learn to wrap you and feed you. She brought me hot pads for my back."

My mother asked the nurse for a very American-sounding name.

"Kevin. Brandon. Dexter," the nurse suggested.

My mother didn't know any of these names. When she tried to repeat them, she saw the nurse wince. She knew she was not pronouncing them well.

"What about Jason?" the nurse asked. "That's my son's name."

My mother looked at the calendar. She saw the months she carried me. July—August—September—October—November—December.

"Yes," she said, training her tongue to mimic the nurse. "He is Jason."

"What about a middle name?"

She looked back at the calendar. December.

Jason D. Riazi. She repeated the foreign name to herself, holding her American baby in her arms. She hoped that this name she could hardly pronounce would protect me, make me untouchable.

"I fall behind in school," my mom explains, continuing the story. "They sent me letters. I tried to explain I need time. You were so small and still in the hospital. Then I got one letter that says I cannot be in this country. The letter tells me I have to leave, but how can I go? My baby is in the hospital and your father's grave is not yet covered in grass. And the people who called our families, they were still calling. They are angry because your father's face was on the front of the newspaper and many people loved him. The bad people, they promise that the country will never be safe for his family."

So she stayed in America.

But with my father dead, what were the chances that they would give his family a visa? Who could she ask without risking being sent back to Afghanistan?

At any point, she could be found. At any point, she could be arrested. She had an expired passport and an expired student visa. That meant that if the authorities found her, they would send her back to Afghanistan. Knowing what happened to my father and the terrible words the people said, she had to make an impossible choice.

She sold all her textbooks and put away her notebooks. She buried her hopes of becoming a doctor and decided to pray for smaller miracles. She went from store to store in town, looking for a job, a new apartment away from the college and ways to disappear.

She didn't get a driver's license. She didn't apply for good jobs. She didn't ask for help from the government even when she worried about how to feed us both. She did what she could to disappear into America and prayed this country would hide us from the evil that had taken my father.

"You need to understand," my mother tells me. Her words are slow and quiet but real. "If they find me, they will tell me to go. But you stay. And if this happens, every breath I take will be to move the mountain between us."

Three

On this November Friday, when there is no school, I refuse to think about what I've learned about my mother and father. I'm determined to enjoy this day off. In the month since my mother's birthday, knowing what my mother has been hiding has left me with a strange feeling. I'm a little ashamed of what she's done and I'm ashamed that I'm ashamed. If my mother's not American, how can I be? But if I've never been to Afghanistan, how can I be Afghan?

That's why I'm really happy for an extra day away from my classmates who have no idea what my mom and I really are—or aren't. There's no school today because it's a professional day for teachers.

"Professional day? How professional is it to skip work?" Mr. Fazio told my mother grumpily last week when she asked if I could stay with her in the laundromat. "But that's fine with me. Jason D can hang out here."

My mother brought Mr. Fazio some home-baked bread the next day as a thank-you. She didn't need to. Mr. Fazio always lets my mother bring me to the shop. She's been working for him for five years, and he always jokes that she somehow makes people want to wash even their clean clothes.

This morning, I want to sleep in but I can't. I squeeze my eyes tight and even try burying my head under my pillow. The smell of cardamom lingers in the apartment, and I know my mother's already up. I hear the distant sound of music, old Afghan songs. I can picture her sitting at our breakfast table, her hands wrapped around a steaming mug of green tea and her dark hair pulled into a ponytail with a few stray curls framing her face. This is the only time of day when she's not moving at full speed. By the time she drains that cup, she'll be charged, ready for a busy day at the laundromat, and I won't see her sit down again until it's time to review my homework. Surely if I think about algebra equations or start counting laundry machines, I'll fall right back asleep.

After five more minutes, I throw the blanket off me in defeat.

I stumble into the kitchen, my eyes half shut in protest.

"Hungry?"

"Not really."

"I could make you something."

"Like what?"

My mother raises an eyebrow.

"A ceramic bowl filled with water of two colors. What am I?"

I may be half asleep but I can still solve her riddles.

"An egg. Too easy."

"Too easy?" she says. "Okay. A golden nail stuck in the ground."

"A carrot."

She furrows her brows, pretending to be annoyed that I've figured it out.

"Forty rooms with forty shelves and forty bulbs."

"Pomegranate."

"He is in the house while his beard is outside."

"An ear of corn."

"A purple robe and a green crown."

I guess my mom's forgotten that she's asked me this one at least ten times before.

"An eggplant."

"Fine, Shah-jan. You know everything. Eat something, and when you get ready, come to the shop."

"Maybe I could stay here instead."

"No."

"Kings are allowed to stay home alone in their castles, Mom." I throw her own words back at her.

"Already we talked about it."

"Mom, please. Just once can't I—"

She lifts a finger. My mother is a strange kind of superhero. Her power? Ending all debate with one finger.

My mom speaks English perfectly well except for a few things. One is that the words are sometimes ordered wrong, kind of like the sentence went into the dryer and got all jumbled. The other thing is that she pronounces words strangely. *Volleyball* is "wolleyball." *Sponge* is "ehsponge." And she mixes up *he* and *she* a lot because in her language there is no *he* or *she*. I didn't notice it when I was younger, but then I did. I saw that the librarian asked her to repeat her question. I saw that the customer service person on the phone did the same. Was the receptionist at my doctor's office annoyed because of mom's accent or some other reason? And once I noticed that my mom talked differently from others, I couldn't un-notice it. It made me wonder if there were other things she was doing differently or . . . well . . . wrong. I wondered if there were things I was doing or saying wrong because I learned them from her.

"But you heard Auntie Seema last night. She says it's no big deal to trust me alone for a few hours and the

23

laundromat is only a fifteen-minute walk from here," I mutter, reluctant to give up completely.

Since it's just my mom and me, Auntie Seema, my mom's best friend, is the one person we turn to when we disagree. Sometimes she thinks I should give my mom a break. That's when my mom smiles and looks at Auntie Seema like she's brilliant. But lots of times Auntie Seema agrees with me. When she does, my mom points out that Auntie Seema is a fifty-something-year-old woman who wears ripped jeans and paisley bandannas tied around her head. And when she decided to move into New York City, my mom decided Auntie Seema was just a little bit out of her mind.

"Auntie Seema is not your mother. He can't make decisions for you."

There she goes again.

"*She* can't make decisions for me."

"Exactly."

"No, you said *he*."

It feels even more important to correct her English now, as if her English mistakes could prove she's wrong about other, bigger things.

"Fine, *she*. But you know what I mean, Jason. Don't make a big deal from the small things."

Auntie Seema gets that the small things are a big deal, but I don't say that out loud.

Auntie Seema was born in India, but she's been American since she was two years old. She and my mom have been friends since before I was born. They met in New Jersey, close to where my mom was going to school. Auntie Seema lived nearby then and taught art at a studio. They were both walking to a bus stop when my mom tripped and stumbled into the street just as a bus was approaching. My mom was pregnant with me at the time. Auntie Seema yanked her back to the sidewalk just in time. Mom says Auntie Seema saved both our lives.

Since India and Afghanistan are next to each other, it was almost like they found long-lost friends in each other. My mother told Auntie Seema that she didn't know any Afghans in America, and that she wanted me to be American. She didn't want me to know the terrible things she'd run away from. Auntie Seema took my mother back to her apartment that day because she looked so scared. She gave my mother a cup of warm chai. She played music my mother had listened to when she was younger and told her everything would be okay, even if America was not made of gold as people back home thought.

Auntie Seema always says smart things. She's one of the only people my mom trusts, even though they're almost nothing alike.

"Why don't you talk to an immigration lawyer?" my mother said Auntie Seema asked her more than once.

"Apply to stay in the country."

"And if they say no? Then they will tell me to leave. It is dangerous for us back home. I can take the chance for me, but how can I make my child take a chance?"

Auntie Seema learned that she can disagree with my mother but it's nearly impossible to change her mind, especially when it comes to me.

"You and the baby won't be alone," Auntie Seema decided. My mother said she saw kindness in Auntie Seema's light-brown eyes and long, artistic fingers. She finished the warm chai.

She looked at the paintings in Auntie Seema's apartment, canvases of all sizes leaning against the walls. There was one of a woman, her arms raised over her head, reaching for the sky.

"It was the most beautiful painting," my mother told me. "Do you know why people look to the sky when they pray, Shah-jan? Do you know why we hang flags so far above our heads? Because we want to touch that sky, the sky that turns from blue to purple to pink and orange. You can find all colors in the sky. The sun, the moon, the stars, and the clouds—it has room for them all. That's why I love this country, my king. It is like the sky at our feet."

My mother stopped crying when she saw Auntie Seema's painting. It reminded her that there might be a place for her somewhere. It reminded her that she had lots to do to get ready for me, and there was no room for tears.

My mother turns off the music playing from her cell phone, unfazed by my argument that the laundromat is a short walk from our apartment.

"Auntie Seema is talking so much about the planet sometimes she is forgetting the people are different from trees." I groan softly, knowing what she's going to say. "You can leave a tree alone. You cannot leave a kid alone."

Yes, Auntie Seema is a tree-hugging artist. She recycles everything, including canvases, sometimes painting over one piece to create a new one. She's a free spirit and the complete opposite of my mom. That's what makes Auntie Seema the most unlikely third person in our lives. While we take turns being disappointed in Auntie Seema's opinions, we both love Auntie Seema to pieces.

My mom goes out the door and I hear her lock it from the outside. I throw some clothes on and brush my teeth. I check myself out in the mirror and yelp when I see one shock of hair sticking straight up. I wet it and do my best to flatten it with the palm of my hand, but it's no use. I can only hope that someday this hairy antenna will prove useful and I'll be the receiver of messages from Mars.

With half a bowl of cereal in my stomach, I leave

the apartment. As promised, I lock the door behind me and walk toward the laundromat. It's been warmer than expected this year. It feels more like September than November, and by the time I get to Bloom Street, I'm thirsty. The vending machine in the laundromat hasn't worked for months, so I walk across the street to the gas station—the one that leaves its giant inflated Santa Claus up year-round—to get a bottle of juice.

I can see my mother from across the street. She is in the laundromat speaking to a customer from behind the counter. Sometimes I sit behind the counter while she cleans the filters of the dryers or sweeps the chipped floor tiles. A stray lint ball can easily pass for a mouse (I've seen three customers shriek and toss their laundry in the air after making this mistake). The air is humid. The sweet scent of fabric softener mixes with the nostril-searing smell of bleach. In the winter, the warmth of the machines makes it one of the best places to be. In the summer, it feels like the entire laundromat is the inside of a dryer, and it's painful.

The soda machine keeps spitting out my crumpled dollar, disgusted. It finally goes through, but only after I press it against the corner of the machine to flatten it. I should go ask my mom to trade me quarters for my bill. Since she works in a laundromat with coin-operated machines, she's always giving customers quarters for their dollars. For my mom's birthday last year, I filled a pencil case with quarters and wrapped it in newspaper. I stuck a red ribbon on top and made a card out of folded construction paper.

Happy birthday to a woman who always makes cents.

She laughed when she shook the package and heard the clinking of coins. *Comedian,* she declared and gave me a playful swat on my shoulder. Even later in the night, I caught her smiling to herself, proud that I had made a clever joke and proud that she understood it.

The two men she's looking at right now are not customers. I can tell because they have no laundry with them. They are wearing identical navy-blue windbreakers and stand with their feet apart. When one turns, I catch a glimpse of a shiny badge hanging around his neck. They are asking questions, looking carefully around the laundromat. The two other women inside stop folding clothes and move closer together. They're watching this happen just as I am. I can see it all, since the sun is hidden behind a cloud and there's no glare. I can see my mother's face, the way she looks from one man to the other. I can see her leaning backward as if she's trying to retreat.

This is bad.

My breathing is quick and shallow, and my palms are sticky with nerves. *This is really bad,* my body's saying.

Run to her, I tell my legs, but they do not listen. *Call her name*, I tell my mouth, but it, too, disobeys.

I don't know exactly what's happening. While my brain's trying to figure it out, my body's reacting like it already knows.

I'm going to regret this moment, I know. I'm going to hate myself for what I'm doing now. Why didn't I tell my mother to call in sick today? Why couldn't I have been sick and needed her to stay home with me? Why didn't I wake up a little earlier and go to the laundromat with her?

I can tell by the way her shoulders are hunched that she's anxious.

I remember the conversation we had on my mom's birthday, just one month ago, and I feel sick to my stomach. It's happening. I wish she hadn't talked about it—maybe speaking it made it true.

I think about doing something heroic. I think about walking across the street, swinging the door open, and sneaking my mom out the laundromat's back door before these guys can even figure out what's happening. I want to swoop in and tell them that they have no right to do this.

But that's not what I do.

Instead, I watch my mother try to explain something to them. I see her point to herself and shake her head. I see her steal a quick glance out the window but only when they have turned their backs to her momentarily. She fumbles through her purse and touches the back of her neck. The men in the blue jackets have asked her to come out from behind the counter. They bring her outside. They don't have their hands on her but they're controlling her movements all the same.

Once she's outside, my mother looks in my direction, and I wonder if she can see me. I don't know how to signal her. There isn't much time for me to figure it out. Mr. Fazio, the owner of the laundromat, has just come down the street. He is shaking his head. He has one hand on his forehead and another on his hip. He stands with the men—they must be some kind of police officers. They ask him something, but he shakes his head again and shrugs his shoulders.

He doesn't help her.

I press myself against the vending machine, its tiny vibrations mixing with the nervous energy in my bones. I want to believe that a twelve-year-old can be a hero, but my gut tells me my mother wants me to stay hidden.

She's on the sidewalk. They are right behind her. She turns her gentle brown eyes back to Mr. Fazio. She crumples for just a half second before she lifts her head and looks around. She's looking for me. She doesn't see me,

but I can see her lips say my name from across the street.
My Shah.

A million times before she's called me her king, but I've never been so desperate to hear it.

I love you, I want to shout, but instead I put a hand over my mouth. One of the men leans into the car and then returns to have another word with Mr. Fazio. They give him some papers. He is still shrugging, bewildered. He's wiping his forehead with a handkerchief. The smooth, hairless center of his head reflects the morning sun. The two women in the laundromat stay so close to the machines they look like they might crawl into them. One of them has a cell phone pressed to her ear. My mother hangs her head low enough to hide her eyes. Sunlight makes her hair shine and, although it's impossible, I can smell her shampoo from here, fruity and sweet. I want to bury my head in her shoulder and feel her hair tickle my cheeks.

Had my mother known? Had she seen this coming? Was she warning me of this moment?

I want to cry when I see her nudged into the back seat of their black car. I want to chase after that car and bang on its windows, slam my fists on its trunk. I want to scream that she's all I have and beg them not to take her, but she's broken a rule. What can I possibly say?

I'm terrified to see my mother being taken away. I want to pull her out of there and hold her hand as we run back to our apartment. I don't do any of that. I'm scared and angry and sad.

I'm a lot of things, but shocked is not one of them, because my mother, on her birthday, told me we could lose each other.

Four

Every breath I take will be to move the mountain between us.

The mountain was invisible until now. With my mother gone, I see the mountain she talked about. It is rising, rising from the ground until it is so big that it blots out the sun.

Mother, I think with my balled hands covering my eyes. *What made you think you could move the earth?*

The black car pulls away. There are no flashing lights or blaring sirens. How could this be? How could my mother be taken from me without the entire world noticing? One of the women inside the laundromat transfers an armful of damp clothes into a dryer. A minivan moves past me with two children in car seats. They are waving toys in the air in some kind of back seat celebration. One of the customers joins Mr. Fazio in the street, and they look all around. I stay concealed behind the soda machine.

I have nothing against Mr. Fazio, but he just let the officers take my mother away, and I don't know what he's going to do if he finds me. With my mother gone, I'm going to have to start making big decisions, and hiding from Mr. Fazio is my first.

What should I do? What *can* I do?

I look down and see that I'm wearing jeans, a green polo shirt, and gray sneakers. I have a few quarters in my pocket and a key to our house tucked into a pocket my mother has sewn into the inside of my jeans after I lost my third key. I do not have a cell phone or a backpack or anything that might be helpful for a kid who is now on his own. I have a bottle of apple juice that I don't want anymore.

What should I do, Mom?

Leaning against the whirring soda machine, I think of the million times I wanted my mother to stop telling me what to do. I slide to the ground and wait for my mother's voice to reach me.

Jan-em, I hear. *I told you this could happen.*

I don't want to cry. I can't risk someone coming around the corner and finding me here in tears. Maybe they would call the police. Would they take me to my mother?

You are American. I am not. I'm not supposed to be here. I don't have papers.

She made it very clear last month what would happen if people with badges ever showed up and asked her to show papers.

I stay in this country. My mother doesn't.

I don't understand how a piece of paper can mean the difference between us being together and us being torn apart. It seems like it should take something a lot scarier or stronger than a piece of paper to do that.

I wipe my face and take a deep breath. Being alone is scary. That's why Auntie Seema didn't want my mother to feel alone. That's why she became family to us.

Auntie Seema.

Suddenly the clouds in my head clear. I need to get to Auntie Seema. I know that she lives in New York City, but I don't know her address.

I push myself off the ground and wipe the seat of my jeans. It's still early, and there aren't as many cars on the road as there will be in a few hours. I've got to get to my aunt. That's what my mother would want me to do. But to get to Auntie Seema is no easy feat. We don't visit her because Mom can't shake the feeling that New York is a dangerous place since the evening news is always report-ing a crime there. It makes Auntie Seema furious to hear

Mom say things like that, but it's one of those things that they forever disagree on. Auntie Seema comes to visit us every couple of months. She takes the train and we meet her at the station, which is a few blocks from our apartment.

I have a plan. I need to get into New York City and find Auntie Seema, but to do that I'm going to need a few things. I've got to go home first. I pray that the men with badges are not there waiting for me.

It takes me only ten minutes to make my way back home. I keep my head low and my hands stuffed in my pockets. I don't know if anyone's looking for me, but I don't want to take any chances. I look out of the corner of my eye when I hear a car whizzing past me, checking to make sure it's not the officers, the guys who took my mother away. When I hear someone shout, my heart flies into a frenzy. It's just a man talking loudly on a cell phone, but my heartbeat takes a long time to recover.

The walk gives me time to think, which is not necessarily a good thing. I've got something scary to do and, I realize as I put one foot in front of the other, it's a lot easier to *do* than *think*. I'm just grateful to be moving, even if I'm not sure I'm going in the right direction.

Ms. Raz is sweeping the front steps of our building. I see her from a distance and take a deep breath. I have to get past her without letting on that something's happened. I'm also not sure if the officers have already been here.

"Jason D," she says when I place my foot on the first step. She adjusts the thin-framed glasses that are forever drifting down her nose. She's been looking at me suspiciously ever since the day she found me on the roof with the pigeons. She hasn't said anything to my mother about it yet, and I don't know if she will.

Ms. Raz learned my name only last year, when I delivered containers of my mother's cooking to her door. She was bedridden after breaking her hip, and the only person coming in or out of her apartment was a nurse who stopped by for one hour each day. She was annoyed that I'd knocked on her door, but took the foil-covered plate all the same. We sent food every day until we saw Ms. Raz walking around outside the way she used to. She told me that day that we didn't have to send food anymore. She wasn't an invalid, she snapped. I asked my mother what an invalid was. My mother wasn't sure, but decided Ms. Raz didn't need any more food. That might be the only reason why she hasn't complained about my being on the roof.

"Everything okay? Mom okay?"

"Hi, Ms. Raz. Everything's good, thanks," I say, trying to keep my voice even and casual as I move up the stairs. "Mom's at work."

Ms. Raz nods approvingly and takes a momentary break, putting a hand on her back and squinting at the morning sun.

"Mom works hard."

I nod in agreement, squeeze my lips into a forced smile, and slip past her before she can ask any other questions.

I walk up the two flights of steps to our apartment. I use the key, warm from being pressed against my hip, to open the door, then I close the door behind me and flip the deadbolt closed too. I run to the window of our living room and steal a glance down at the street. No one's followed me, and there are no threatening-looking cars around. I look at our home and it suddenly feels like a museum full of artifacts from a former life.

The pictures on our bookshelf are portraits. The dishes my mom left drying on the rack are an exhibit. What will happen to all of our stuff? What will happen to our home? I can't think about it too much. *Doing is better*, I remind myself. *Keep doing and moving.*

I walk into the room I share with my mother. We used to share one big bed, but two years ago I raised a fuss, asking for my own bed. I came home from school to find our queen-size bed had been replaced with two twin beds. I felt pretty cool to finally have my own bed. Then again, I always end up in Mom's bed whenever I get sick, even if it's just a case of the sniffles.

I pull my backpack out of my closet and stuff a change of clothes in it. Then I open the plastic frames and take the photograph of my father in his gray shirt and the one with his laughing friend. Next, I take the picture of my mother holding a one-year-old me on her lap in a grassy park. I tuck them between the pages of a small notebook and slip them into my backpack.

In the kitchen, I open a cabinet and take out the small tin that used to hold tea leaves. This is the money my mom has given me for the occasional ice cream cone. I pull out a small bunch of one-dollar bills and a few coins and stuff them into the pocket of my pants. I pick up the strainer I've knocked off the counter in my haste and hold it in my hands.

Drops of rain fall from my sky full of stars. What am I?

I lift the strainer over my head. It is a metal sky, light shining through the holes like twinkling stars.

This one took me a while to figure out but I did it. How I'm going to get to Auntie Seema's house is a much more complicated puzzle, but I'll figure it out too.

Auntie Seema.

I run back into my bedroom and dig through my shoes to get to a cardboard box. I fold the flaps back into place and find the return address. Auntie Seema sent me a pair of sneakers for my birthday, and I kept the box because it's not too often that I get packages addressed to me, Mr.

Jason D. Riazi. On the top left corner is half of Auntie Seema's name and her address. I tore part of it when I ripped the tape off the box that day, eager to see what my aunt had sent me.

74th St., Apt. B5
New York, New York

I tear off the square with her address on it and feel a rush as I stuff it into the front pocket of my backpack. I'm a little less afraid now that I have an address, but I'm also a little more afraid because I don't know if I'll make it to this address.

Just keep moving, I tell myself. *Stop thinking.*

Back in the kitchen, I toss three granola bars and a juice box into my backpack, then pause for a moment. I don't know if I'll ever see this place again. I don't know if I'll ever see my mother again. I don't know if I'll actually be able to find my aunt. I don't know much at all.

I look at the blue-and-gray sofa, the sun-faded curtain over the kitchen window, and the small bowl of potpourri that stopped smelling like anything three years ago. I look at the hook where I sometimes but not always remember to hang my jacket, and the kitchen chair where my mother sets her handbag. There's a green line on the wall from when I tripped holding an open green marker. There's the fridge full of my mother's cooking: stewed okra, white rice with cumin, and meatballs.

"Good-bye," I whisper with my back pressed against the door to the small but perfect world that was my mother and me. And while I don't know much, there is one thing I know for sure. As soon as my mother's feet hit Afghanistan, she'll find a way for us to be together again. All I've got to do is be somewhere that she'll find me.

Five

I adjust the straps of the backpack on my shoulders and make it down the steps and out of the building without seeing Ms. Raz. Each step feels like a thousand. Am I doing the right thing?

I'm passing by the bagel store where my mother sometimes gets us breakfast.

"Hey, there! Kid!"

My heart leaps into my throat. The voice is coming from behind me. I consider running but turn my head just a bit so I can see if the voice belongs to someone in a blue windbreaker.

"Where do you think you're going?"

An elderly man is waving a finger at me. I want to keep

walking, but my mother would lose her mind if she saw me ignoring someone that age. The man has just come out of a shoe repair shop and is shaking his head. He's not one of the blue-jacket men, but I'm still ready to make a dash.

"Run while you can," he mumbles, his hands trembling in a steady rhythm. "Are you skipping school?"

"No, sir. There's no school today," I reply nervously.

"No school," he mutters and taps his cane angrily on the sidewalk. "Kids have it so easy these days. Nothing to worry about except video games and cell phones. When I was young . . ."

He walks away from me, heading back into the shoe repair shop. That's when I feel something grab at the back of my jeans, right around my calves. I yelp and my backpack falls off my shoulders. There's a small dog tied to a parking meter. I back up so he can't jump on me again. He's perched on my backpack, barking triumphantly.

"Hey, that's my bag!" I reach over to pick the bag up but pull my hand away when his jaw snaps at me.

"I need that!" I say desperately. I reach over again but this time the dog flashes me a sharp-toothed warning.

I take a step back. He looks angry, as if I've threatened him instead of the other way around.

"What's going on out there, troublemaker?"

Someone is coming to the door of a shop. I don't want

to be forced to explain where I'm going or why I'm not in school. The door starts to swing open, sending a bell dinging. As if the bell was a signal, I take off, racing down to the end of the block and turning the corner. I put my hands on my knees, panting, and peek around the corner. The sidewalk is empty.

I let out an angry groan. How could I have lost my backpack already? I kick at the wall and take a deep breath. I need to put distance between me and this place. The train station is still a few blocks away. At least I have the money in my pocket. I close my eyes for a second to picture the cardboard scrap I'd put into my backpack and burn Auntie Seema's address into my brain.

74th St., Apt. B5
New York, New York

The train will take me to Auntie Seema's apartment in New York City, a place my mother refused to go out of fear. That means I have to be even braver than her. On the other hand, if I don't do this, I could end up lost or picked up by the police for being without a mom. That's a lot scarier than going to New York City, so maybe I'm not brave. Maybe I'm just choosing between being afraid and being more afraid.

The train station has a wide entrance. I walk in along with a handful of other people. No one's paying attention to me so far, but I'm still anxious.

There are platforms on both sides. I've heard Auntie Seema talk about getting a train ticket, so I know I'll need one. I look at the ticket booth and see a woman sitting inside. She looks annoyed to be there, and I can see why. I wouldn't want to sit in a glass box all day either.

My palms are sweaty, so I wipe them on my jeans before I get in line to approach her. Will she sell a ticket to a kid alone, or will she call the cops?

She could call the cops and I could get taken away. What do they do with kids who don't have parents? I think of the orphanage from the movie our music teacher made us watch. That girl with the big curly hair did everything she could to get away from that place. I don't feel much like singing or dancing when I think of it, so I step out of the line and look around. Maybe I can just run onto the train? If I get caught, I'll go straight to jail for breaking the law, so that idea isn't a very good one.

C'mon, Jason D, I tell myself. *Figure this out.*

That's when I spot three blue-and-orange machines along the side wall. There's a sign above them with letters big enough that I can read from where I stand: *TICKETS*. I walk over to the machines, stealing a quick glance over my shoulder to be sure the ticket booth lady isn't watching me.

The machine has a huge touch screen, kind of like the world's biggest tablet. I follow the directions and purchase a one-way ticket to the last stop, New York City. I keep sliding one-dollar bills into the machine until it spits out a ticket. That leaves me with only a few coins, but I can't think about that now.

I've seen Auntie Seema's apartment once. She texted my mother a picture of herself standing in front of her home, a narrow building with a Dominican restaurant on the ground level and two apartments over it. Auntie Seema's apartment is the very top one, my mother told me. In the photograph, there are hulking concrete buildings with narrow windows along the block. When my mother would let me use her phone, I would look at that picture and try to imagine what it would be like to visit Auntie Seema in New York City.

I take my ticket and try to look as confident as I can, pulling my shoulders back and keeping my eyes straight ahead. I follow the crowd and move to the platform for the train that goes to New York. There are people in jackets and polished shoes with work bags slung over their shoulders all moving toward one platform to wait for the train. I know they're going to New York City because they are so dressed up.

There's a man in a business suit pacing the platform. He's got an earpiece in one ear and is deep into a conversation. He barely notices the annoyed looks he's getting from the people around him. I make my way over to him and stand near enough that I could touch his black trench coat or his leather briefcase.

When the train pulls into the station, he doesn't notice me follow close behind him, taking the middle when he slides into the window seat. He's ignoring everyone else here, which is why I think he'll ignore me too.

I keep my fingers crossed and sigh with relief when a woman takes the aisle seat next to me. I'm sandwiched between two adults who both look like they've got lots on their mind. This is exactly what I needed. Mr. Talk-a-lot spends the entire ride chatting about stuff like "sales projections" and "the satellite team in Dallas" and "quarterly reports." The woman on my right takes out her laptop and lets out an exaggerated sigh as she puts in her earbuds. She shoots Mr. Talk-a-lot a look and turns up the volume on her phone to drown him out.

The train starts moving. The man and woman next to me are each holding passes in plastic covers. I sneak a look around and see a man slide a paper ticket like mine into the small pocket in the seat in front of him. I do the same, though my ticket is a little crumpled and splotchy from my clammy palms.

I close my eyes and pretend to sleep. It's the best way I can think of to avoid conversation. I've done the same thing at home when my mother's asking me to get out of bed or if I've finished my reading homework.

When I feel someone standing over us, I open my eyelids just enough that I'm seeing the world through my eyelashes. I see the train conductor pick up the paper tickets, punch holes in them with a metal clicker, and replace them into the seat tabs. I should relax then, knowing my plan has worked well so far, but I can't. I keep thinking about my mom, wondering where she is and how soon they'll send her back to Afghanistan. I wonder if she's on her way to the airport now. I want to scream and punch the seat in front of me.

Sometimes it takes a whole lot of energy to do something, and sometimes it takes even more energy to do nothing. I usually hate the days I'm trapped in the laundromat with my mother, but right now I would give anything to be staring at laundry spinning in circles.

Today is upside down and inside out and nothing makes sense.

I spend the thirty-seven-minute ride thinking about it while I fake-sleep. The two people on either side of me don't notice that I never speak to either of them. Each assumes I am traveling with the other. When the train pulls into the last stop, Penn Station, I join all the other passengers in shuffling out the train doors. I'm in the city now and about to start the second part of my mission.

My head is dizzy with questions. My stomach growls, angry that I ate only half a bowl of cereal this morning.

As the swarm of people moves into the grand corridor with its flittering arrival and departure boards, no one notices that I slowly drift away from Mr. Talk-a-lot and the annoyed laptop lady. No one notices me as I stand in the center of the train station and try not to look as scared as I feel.

I need to stay focused. I've got to get to Seventy-Fourth Street. I don't know how I'm going to do that, but I'm hoping to find some signs when I get out onto the street. I see more people than I've ever seen before. They are moving in all directions. My breaths quicken. I jump when I feel someone bump into me, and I don't feel any better when I hear a mumbled apology.

I see a police officer scanning the station and wonder if he's looking for me.

Suddenly, my head starts to feel like a balloon drifting away from its string. The features of the people walking past me go fuzzy. The police officer is gone. A thick black curtain drops over my eyes. I feel my knees fold. I don't know what's happening, but I do know there's no way to fight it. The dark world has gone darker.

And down I go.

Six

*M*y head hurts. That's all I know. There's a low hum of voices in the background, but I can't make out the words. Only one whisper breaks through like the thin light of the moon in a dark sky. I have to strain to hear it.

If you have me, you want to share me.

It sounds like a riddle. I know the answer—I just can't think of it. The whisper is persistent.

If you have me, you want to share me. If you share me, you haven't got me.

As if someone's got a finger on the volume button, the voices in the background get louder. I still don't know where I am.

Gown. Scanner. Oxygen. Those are the words I pick up

with interest, like unbroken shells on a sandy beach.

The humming around me now includes a rhythmic beeping. My pointer finger is heavy. It takes a lot of effort to lift that finger only to have it drop again. It's weighed down by something.

If you have me, you want to share me. If you share me, you haven't got me.

Now I'm panicking. My head—why is it throbbing? I start to remember then: the train station and that funny way the world went dark.

"There you are, hon. You've had a concussion, but don't you worry. You're going to be just fine. We're taking care of you. Can you tell me your name?"

I bend my knee and let out a moan.

"Can you tell me your name, sweetheart? Tell me your name, darling. Can you do that?"

If you have me, you want to share me. If you share me, you haven't got me.

The whisper hasn't gone away.

"Come on. Tell us your name."

I can't do that. My shoulder blades press against the bed. I squint, the lights over me shining whiter than truth.

"Urgh." That is all I can say. It is not my most eloquent moment.

"Poor thing. Help us out, sweetheart, so we can call your parents. Surely someone's going crazy looking for you."

I blink, my eyelids heavy as stones. I'm in a hospital gown. Blue with red stars. Where are my clothes? I groan, embarrassed as I realize that a stranger got me out of my clothes and into this Fourth-of-July gown.

Someone tosses a few sheets of paper onto my knees.

"Poor thing. The bed's ready for him upstairs. There's his chart. He's Manhattan Doe for now until he can tell us his name."

Manhattan Doe? Manhattan Doe sounds like a name a celebrity would give her kid, and I'm surely not the child of a celebrity.

I hear the high-pitched squeal of a wonky wheel. My head hurts and I'm cold. I wish I could ask for a blanket, but I still can't get my tongue to do anything useful.

There's the ding of an elevator. Through half-open eyes, I see the metal doors slide open. My escort spins my bed around and rolls me in, headfirst. I watch the doors close.

The woman touches a hand to my shoulder.

"You're going to be all right, hon. Don't be scared, okay? They're going to take real good care of you upstairs, and when you're feeling a little more together, you can tell your nurse what your name is and where we can find your family."

If you have me, you want to share me. If you share me, you haven't got me.

This nice woman is doing her best to make me feel

more comfortable, but she's going about it all wrong. It's not her fault. I haven't really given her much information to go on.

There's a ding, and three other people join me in the elevator. A woman is being pushed in a wheelchair by a man in scrubs. The man in scrubs gives me a nod. The woman is wearing a bathrobe over her hospital gown, and in her arms there's a newborn baby wrapped up in a white blanket with pink and blue stripes. I can't see its face but it looks pretty cozy. The mother gives me one of those uncomfortable smiles and turns back to her baby, adjusting the blanket around its chin.

I turn my eyes back to the ceiling of the elevator and try not to think about how tightly this woman is holding her baby—like she'll never let it be taken away from her. The woman pushing my stretcher winks at the new mother beside us and whispers congratulations. Then she gives my shoulder a little squeeze.

There's another ding.

"This is our floor, hon." With one push, I'm rolled out of the elevator. I swear I can almost hear that new mother let out a sigh of relief, as if she can't wait to get her baby away from me and whatever bad luck or germs I carry. We go down a hallway so fast that the signs on the walls are blurry. We pause so the woman can hit a metal button commanding double doors to open and let us into the pediatric ward of the hospital. I'm rolled into a room with glass doors, and another nurse appears at my bedside.

"This is Manhattan Doe?"

"Yup."

"And still not recalling his name or nothing?"

"Not unless the elevator ride jogged his memory. Hon, you remember your name now?"

If you share me, you haven't got me.

When I don't answer, they go back to talking to each other.

"All right, sweetness, let's get you tucked in."

The beeping starts up again, and it's not helping my headache. Then again, my headache probably has more to do with all the questions I know are going to keep coming my way.

What were you doing at the train station? Where is your mother?

How will I answer these questions? How will I ever get to Auntie Seema now? Maybe this is the end. Maybe they're going to figure out what I've done and send me to a place for kids without parents.

How could I have let this happen? I've put it all together now—the half bowl of cereal, the running to the train station, the panic of being in what looked like the world's busiest train station. I passed out and thumped my head on the floor.

The nurse doesn't notice the tear slide down my cheek. She doesn't hear the quiet whisper that's in my head.

If you have me, you want to share me. If you share me, you haven't got me. What am I?

I answer under my breath. *I know what you are,* I say. *You're a secret.*

The whisper is telling me what I need to do. I'm not going to answer the questions coming my way. I'm going to find a way out of here. I didn't think getting to Auntie Seema would be easy, but I also didn't think it would be this hard. I'm not ready to give up, though. I'm going to follow that whisper's advice and keep the secret of who I am.

The nurse picks up the papers that were resting on my knees and flips through them quickly. She turns her focus back to me and wipes the corner of my mouth with a soft paper towel. "Looks like you're coming out of it already," she observes, and I have to admit her voice is pretty soothing. "We'll move you to a regular room then. In the meantime, see if you can come up with your real name, okay? I don't like Manhattan Doe. It sounds like the kind of name a celebrity would give her kid."

Seven

I haven't spent a night in a hospital since those first
months after I was born. Last night was my first night
here, though I don't remember much of it. I was groggy
and confused most of the time and my head is just starting to clear. The hospital smells funny—kind of clean and
kind of stuffy all at once. And there are lots of sounds.
There's always a machine beeping, doors clunking shut,
carts and stretchers rolling around.

I'm in a small room with wide windows. I have an
adjustable bed with the top half elevated so I'm sitting
more than lying down. The bed has thick side rails on
either side. There's a flat-screen television mounted on the
wall across from me and a side table beside me with a cup

of water and a telephone. The door has a small window so I can see into the hallway.

For the past hour, I've been staring at the phone. Do I dare? I slip my arm through the handrail and reach for the receiver. I can hear the dial tone.

I don't know where my mother might be right now. I want to call her, but I'm scared that the police will pick up and track me down. Still, the thought of hearing my mother's voice makes me bold enough to risk it. I look at the phone.

For outside calls, dial 9 first.

My fingers are trembling as I press the numbers, and even more when her cell phone starts to ring. It feels like the receiver is growing hot in my hand, and I'm ready to throw it away.

On the fourth ring, someone picks up. I wait for the voice, holding my breath.

"Hello?" It's a man's voice. "Hello?"

My mother always answers her phone. Why? Because it might be me. I think of all the times I've called her. Sometimes she picks up just to tell me she can't talk and will call me back in a moment. Sometimes when she answers I can hear an echo and I know that she's got her head inside one of the machines. Sometimes when she picks up she's out of breath, and I know that she ran for the phone, afraid I might be in trouble and need her. This is the first time I can remember that she hasn't answered, and that makes me sick to my stomach.

"Hello?"

There's an urgency in the man's voice now. I remember the men who led my mother into their car. I hang up the phone without saying a word. My head lands on the pillow, and I slam my fists against the mattress.

Now I've really lost her.

The next couple of hours pass painfully. My scalp is throbbing; a tender lump has formed where my head hit the floor in the train station. I still haven't said much to the nurse who keeps coming in to check on me. She'll have to keep calling me "sweetness" for now.

"Hey there, buddy." In comes a doctor in light-green scrubs and a white coat. Her long black hair is held back in a ponytail, and she's wearing a silver necklace with a pendant in the shape of a horseshoe. She's got a stethoscope slung around the back of her neck. "I'm Dr. Shabani."

Normally, this is where I would respond with my name, but life is not normal right now. I let her friendly gesture hang there, unreturned.

"So, anything you want to share . . . ?"

Her voice trails off like she's waiting for me to jump in and say it's all come back to me. Just then I spot two women with name tags clipped to their shirt pockets. A second later, I see the face of a nurse with red hair. They all steal glances into this room from the hallway.

I shrug and shake my head.

"Okay, don't worry about it," she says as she squeezes my hand.

I don't want this doctor or anyone here to think I'm dumb. I take a deep breath and hope nothing I say gets me in trouble.

"Good to see you awake. Do you know what day it is?"

"Saturday?"

"That's right. And do you know where you are now?"

"A hospital."

"Right. Do you know why?"

"I think I blacked out."

"Yup. Knocked your head on the ground in the train station too."

I touch the side of my head. The lump feels as big as an egg and hurts more when I touch it.

"Yup, right there," the doctor states. She shines a penlight in my eyes, then helps me swing my legs to the side of the bed. She pulls a reflex hammer from the pocket of her white coat and taps on my right knee. My foot jumps out. She does the same to my left, and I wonder if she's ever gotten kicked doing this.

"Shrug your shoulders. Puff out your cheeks. Touch your nose and then my finger. Stick out your tongue."

She makes me get out of bed and balance on one foot, then the other. I'm wearing undies and a hospital gown that flaps open in the back, so when she asks me to walk, heel to toe, across the room, I sidestep like a crab. She asks me to close my eyes and hold my arms straight out.

"It's okay," she says, and taps my shoulder for me to open my eyes. "We'll take it slow. We're all working on it, and we're going to do everything we can to find your mother."

My mother.

She has no idea what that promise does to me. I'm flipping out on the inside and hoping my outside doesn't show it.

I look through the rectangular window and see a nurse in violet scrubs walk past my room and over to the half-moon desk in the center of the hallway where there's a huddle of computers. The rooms are on either side of that large desk area. There are no hiding places here.

"There's something you should know about hospital cafeterias—they're not good. Don't tell anyone I said so, though. I don't recommend this often, but sometimes vending machines are the way to go. How about a bag of pretzels to get something into you for now?"

"I don't think I'll remember. Not even with a bag of pretzels," I say, guessing that this is some kind of trick to get me to talk.

"I didn't think you would," Dr. Shabani says softly. I slide back onto the bed, wondering why I wore my SpongeBob underwear today of all days.

"But even if you don't remember the details," she says slowly, "you might still remember feelings. How do you feel when you think about home? Does it feel like home was a happy place or a sad place? Do you remember if you felt safe there?"

She wants to know if I ran away from a scary home. I think about the pieces of my home. Fried egg and cheese sandwiches on my plate. My blue water bottle filled with mango juice. The five-dollar bill I get only on Fridays to buy pizza in the school cafeteria. My mom humming along to pop music on the radio even when she doesn't know the lyrics. The bowls of raisins and walnuts we share tucked under a comforter on winter days. The pigeons I secretly feed on our roof.

"Hey, are you all right?" Dr. Shabani repeats, breaking my train of thought. "It's something I need to ask. Did you feel safe at home?"

The word *home* jolts me like a speed bump. I search my brain for an answer to Dr. Shabani's simple and complicated question.

But I'm struck with a thought that would knock me off my feet if I weren't already sitting. My mother and I have something in common now. For both of us, home became a place that hurt us, that took away the person we love most.

Eight

There's a quick knock on the door.

"Hey, guy. I'm Eric, and I'm your nurse." Eric doesn't look much older than the high school kid who lives next door to us.

"Hey, Eric."

"I'm gonna check your vitals. Is that cool?"

"Yeah, sure," I say, not wanting to admit I don't know what vitals are. I like how he talks to me—like he's just offered me a soda or chips. No big deal.

"It's your second day here, and it's my second day," Eric announces. "And I'm off to a good start getting assigned to you. You, Mr. Manhattan Doe, are becoming quite famous on this unit."

Eric shines a light in my eyes then peeks at the lump on my head.

"Thanks for going easy on the new guy," Eric says with a laugh. He types something into the computer stationed in the corner of my room. "I'll be back later to check on you. And if you're up to it, you should check out the Reserve."

"The Reserve?"

"Yeah, it's an activity room. We've got some video games and books and puzzles and I don't know what else in there."

"Why's it called the Reserve?"

"Because it's a place for kids to feel like they can take a break from all this hospital stuff. No docs or nurses allowed."

The Reserve is just what I need, especially since a step out of this room is a step in the right direction.

I stand at my door and spot the big room across the hall with decals of Disney characters the size of small children on the windows. There are sheets of paper taped to the door, a collection of finger-painting projects.

I put on a second gown Eric left for me, and this one covers my back. Now that SpongeBob is safely out of sight, I can take a look at the Reserve. It's a room for babies, I'm thinking even as I drag my feet across the hall. I'm pretty sure I'll be miserable in there too, but at least I'll be alone.

I walk into the room and see a car-racing game on a

big-screen television. When I close the door behind me, the game pauses.

"Who *dares* to disturb my game?" roars a voice from the other side. When I don't answer, the armchair swivels around, and what I see makes my jaw drop. In one heartbeat, I'm pressing my back against the closed door and wondering if I've just made another mistake.

"What's your name?" says a girl about my age with a white knit cap over her head. From underneath the cap, a ponytail made of electric wiring hangs out. The wires lead into a small backpack she's got at her side. She looks like some kind of robot.

I can't seem to answer. A polite voice in my head tells me to at least close my gaping mouth.

The girl cocks her ear toward me as if that will help her hear what I've not said. Her chestnut eyes look at me expectantly.

"I only asked you for your name, dude, not how to calculate the speed of light. Still stumped?" She's snappy and smart, which makes me fumble for words.

"Hey, I'm . . . uh . . ."

"O-kay," she says finally. "I'll start. My name is Max."

"Hey."

By now I'm starting to collect myself. Max is wearing a hospital gown too, but she's got purple warm-up pants underneath and a matching sweatshirt on top.

"You know what?" Max says brightly. "It's been really nice getting to know you, but what do you say we take a break from all this talking. Wanna play?"

"Sure," I reply, and watch her swivel her chair back to the television screen with one push of her feet. Her hands are wrapped in white bandages with only her fingers poking through. She looks a little like an unraveling mummy.

"Grab that controller. It's in the basket by the wall."

I spot the basket and walk over toward it. As I do, I catch a glimpse of a uniformed person standing at the half-moon desk in the center of the hallway. It's a police officer.

My breath catches in my throat. Max is staring at me curiously. She follows my gaze and spies the police officer just as a nurse begins nodding at him.

Max looks back at me. "That crafts closet is big enough to hold two football players. Just saying," she mutters, and turns back to the video screen.

Don't think. Just move.

I open the oak cabinet and, just as Max promised, there's more than enough room between the buckets of Lego bricks and rolling carts with drawing supplies to fit me. I close the door behind me and wonder how I can possibly think I'll get away with this.

I hear the door to the Reserve open.

"Hey, sweetie," calls a sugary voice. "Have you seen a

boy in here? This officer's looking to speak with him."

I don't know Max at all. How do I know she isn't pointing at the cabinet this very second?

"There was a dude here but he never told me his name. I think he went to the cafeteria or to get some X-rays of his elbow or something."

"Well, that doesn't make any . . ." The nurse sounds puzzled. "All right, well, thanks."

I hear the door close.

"You're clear," Max calls out. My heart's hammering in my chest, but she's cool as ice cream. I open the door slowly and come back into the Reserve. The hallway outside is empty, and I wonder where the officer and the nurse have gone.

"Ready to play?" Max asks. There's not a hint of worry in her voice.

"Thanks for doing that."

Max shrugs. "It's my special talent. No big deal."

I keep looking at the door, expecting the police officer to come bursting through. Max has pulled out a second controller in the meantime. She hands it to me.

Max chooses the yellow Ferrari as her avatar. I choose a red Corvette. A checkered flag waves and our cars speed off, zipping down virtual city streets and jumping over police cars.

"You're not bad," Max observes.

"Thanks. You play this a lot?"

"First time."

We're both narrowly escaping collisions and are neck and neck in our race to catch up with the white van full of money. The van swerves and turns through narrow streets, green bills flying out the back every time its back doors swing open and closed.

"Dude, watch your back!"

Max wins twice, but in the third game, I corner the white van while she drives off a bridge and falls into the river. She groans, drops the controller, and lets her head slump between her knees in defeat. I look over and see that her wire ponytail collects in a small backpack at her side. I can't figure what all that is for, so I ask.

"What are those wires?"

"What wires?" Max says, looking confused. For a second I regret asking. I should have known better than to pry. But then Max weaves her fingers through her robotic braid. She lowers her voice and looks at the floor. "Oh, you mean *these* wires."

"Sorry, I didn't mean to . . ."

"It's all right," she says. She's sitting straight up again, her knees together as she leans in to tell me her secret. "I'll tell you if you can keep it to yourself. I don't share this personal information with just anyone."

I nod and wait for her to go on.

"These wires are measuring my brain activity. I'm here for specialized testing because, according to the experts, I'm a genius."

"A genius?"

"Yes, a genius," she says with a sigh. "Just something I have to live with. Meanwhile, everyone's interested in finding out how the *magic* happens."

She waves her hands around her head as if a rabbit is going to pop out of her ears.

"What about you?" she asks, her posture relaxing. "Why are you here?"

I look back to the television screen, which is split in two by a flashing lightning bolt. Our cars are on either side of the electric divide, but my Corvette is flashing victoriously.

I'm not a genius. If I were, I probably wouldn't be trapped in this hospital. I barely know this girl and don't dare tell her my real story, even if I am feeling totally alone.

"It's a long story."

Just then the door to the Reserve opens again.

"There you are!"

I turn around to see an open-armed nurse in violet scrubs. Behind her stands a police officer. From the grim look on his face, I can only gather that the Reserve is no longer my safe zone.

Nine

The officer's gold badge gleams bright in my room. My mother was always nervous around police officers, and I never understood why. She wouldn't even cross at an empty crosswalk if the signal didn't give her permission.

His name is Officer Khan. We're back in my hospital room, and he's taken a seat in the visitor's chair across from my bed. He's clean-shaven with thick, dark eyebrows and grayish eyes. He's got his elbows on the armrests and is holding a small notepad in one hand. So far, he hasn't written anything down, because I've told him the same thing I've told everyone else: I can't remember my name, address, phone number, or the names of my parents.

"You were in Penn Station. Do you remember taking the train to get there? Or were you there to get on the train?"

"You know, sir, I really wish I could answer your questions, but the thing is . . ." His badge is really intimidating. My voice sounds funny, a little higher pitched than usual.

"What about your father?"

"No," I say, and I leave it at that.

There's a buzzing sound, and Officer Khan takes his phone out. He raises a finger to tell me he'll only be a moment. He turns his back to me, and I let out a sigh of relief.

I look at the door of my room and see part of a familiar face in the glass window. It's Max. She's peering in, trying not to stick her entire head in the window. When my eyes meet hers, she gives a friendly wave. She points to herself and then into the room, as if to ask if she should enter.

I shake my head no, not sure why she wants to come in here. Officer Khan is now looking at me with raised eyebrows, and I try not to stare at the window. Did he ask a question?

"Okay, let's try something else. When's your birthday?"

Over Officer Khan's shoulder, I see Max waving her bandaged hand around wildly. She's pointing at her head now. She's wincing as if in pain. She holds her head in both hands and presses her lips together tightly. Then she points at me, her face bright with energy. She wants me to act like I'm in pain.

I feel like a genius should be able to come up with a better idea than this. Then again, I don't have any ideas of my own at this second.

I put my hand on my head, right over the lump. I inhale dramatically as Officer Khan tries to become my friend.

"You know, when I was your age, I would sometimes get so angry with my parents that I would wish I had another family. I even thought about running away from home. Every kid's thought about running away from home at one point or another. But I grew up and realized that home's actually the perfect place to be. At least it was for me."

I can tell that he's trying to get me to tell him I ran away from home. I groan softly and close my eyes, my hands still on my head.

"And no matter what was going on in my life, I always found someone to talk to. I would either talk to a cousin or my mom or my best friend at school. That's why I wanted to become a police officer, actually, because I knew how much it helped to just . . . just be there and listen to someone. And that's what I do now. I listen to people and see if I can make things better."

"I am trying. I really am. But when I try to remember anything, it makes my head—"

"Maybe if we look at a map?"

Max opens the door. I stop groaning and watch Officer Khan turn his attention to her.

"The nurse will be in soon with your constipation medicine," Max says cheerfully.

I feel my face flush.

"I just got mine and all I can tell you is it works fast. And by fast, I mean FAST."

Max smiles politely, her eyes sparkling with innocence. It's impressive. Officer Khan is looking for words. When his phone rings a second time, he looks relieved. He steps outside the room to take the call, and Max and I watch him through the window.

"I'm not sure why you keep doing this for me," I say to Max.

"I hate for my talents to go to waste."

Officer Khan opens the door and steps back in.

"Okay, I've got something I need to take care of, but don't worry, I'll be back. If you do remember anything, please let someone here know so they can give me a call. We really want to get you home, kiddo."

I nod, and Officer Khan disappears. I walk to the window ledge. Stale air and dust mites come through the vent. Even in the evening, the sidewalk outside is crawling with people. Some have their hands in their pockets, some walk with a bounce in their step, some wear headphones, some are walking with a friend. Two chubby legs kick playfully in a stroller. A man in a wheelchair holds out a cup as people walk by.

A car tries to move through a crosswalk. The people passing in front of it wave wildly at the driver. One person knocks on the hood of the car and the driver honks back, a warning. Everything and everyone is moving quickly.

Even if I'm sure to be trampled on the way, I've got to get to Auntie Seema's apartment, and all I have is the part of her address I remember from the cardboard box.

I realize that Max is sitting beside me. She's written something into a small notebook with the letter *M* on the cover. She closes it softly and tucks it onto her lap.

"There are lots of good places to hide in a big city," she says slowly. "Lots of places better than a hospital. Want to tell me why you're here?"

I keep my eyes on the city for so long that my eyes start to blur. The bustling street becomes more and more frightening the longer I stare. How am I going to do this alone?

"Max," I say with my eyes on the world outside. "Can you keep a secret?"

Ten

When I finish telling my story, Max is quiet. Her eyes stay on the pale-gray floor tiles. I haven't known her long, but this seems unlike her.

"Sorry, you probably think I'm—"

"Brave." She looks up and faces me. "Even though I don't like that word. But you really are, Jason D."

Now it's my turn to be quiet. I feel a lot of things, but I don't feel brave. It was probably risky to spill my secret, but I feel a lot better now that someone's called me by my real name.

"So that's why the cop was here. Can you get arrested for hiding your real name?"

I shrug. "I don't know. But I need to get out of the

hospital. I'm afraid they'll put me in an orphanage or something."

"An orphanage? Jeez. I see why you want to get out of here. But busting out of a locked hospital unit?"

"There's got to be a way," I say with more determination than I feel. I am a riddle solver, but this is one riddle that has me stumped. How do I get past the nurses and doctors, and the locked door at the end of the hallway, and make my way down nine floors to get out of the building?

"If you've got a plan for this, I need to hear it. There's no way I'm jumping in on some lame plan that's only going to get us caught."

I stare at Max, her mouth pulled to the side in a half smile. Did I hear her correctly?

"What are you talking about?"

"I want to get out there too. There are lots of cool places in the city, like Chinatown and the Central Park Zoo and the Museum of Natural History. . . ."

"You've been to all those places?"

"Not exactly," Max says, a hint of defeat in her voice. "Since we got to New York City, I haven't been anywhere but this hospital. Do you want to hear something totally unfair? My parents are staying in a hotel room that overlooks Central Park, and where am I? Stuck in this hospital with all this junk."

Max points her thumb at the white cap covering her

head of wires. There's a small crack in her voice but the set of her jaw makes her look defiant and strong. I don't know if she's telling the truth about her genius testing, but there is something honest in what she's telling me now. I can see it in her face.

"When I grow up, I want to fly all over the world. I want to go to every single country and try to learn a bunch of different languages and eat lots of different kinds of food. My mom told me she was a foreign exchange student when she was in high school. She lived in Spain for a year with a family. And that family sent their daughter to live in New York with my grandparents. That's what I want to do—maybe in Morocco or Germany or Brazil."

People in my neighborhood would laugh to hear Max talk about other countries as if they're Disneyland.

"What's wrong with staying in America?"

Where I come from, everyone wants to be in the United States. Customers in the laundromat talk about "green cards" and "papers" that give them permission to stay in the United States. People like my mom even break rules to stay in the country. I feel a little flush of embarrassment creep into my cheeks when I think about it. It's still hard to get over.

"There's nothing wrong with staying in America," Max says, her eyes turning to the window. "It's just that America's boring, especially where I live. I want to see something . . . something . . . different."

She says "different" in a dreamy, breathless kind of voice. Then it's her turn to ask me a question.

"Have you ever gone to Afghanistan?"

I shake my head. "Nope."

"Why not?" asks Max.

"My mom said it wasn't safe." I asked my mother once if we would ever go to Afghanistan to visit her family there. My mom looked like she'd just been poked in the heart. She hoped we would, she said, but not now. Given the sad way she said "not now," she might as well have said "never."

"But you're from another country, so it's different for you. I bet you eat different foods and speak a different language and all that. You're not plain old American."

I never thought any of that made me more interesting. I always thought that's what made me strange compared to other American families. Max glides her finger along the buttons of my television remote. Am I glad Max doesn't think we're plain? Sure—but what about being American?

Max sighs deeply. I don't argue with her because I feel like this is an idea she's been working on for a long time, an intricate idea she's carved out of a block of wood.

"For now, all I wanted to do was see New York City. At least New York City isn't as blah as where I live."

"Maybe your parents are going to take you around the

city when you're done with your, um, testing."

Max scoffs at my suggestion. "That's not going to happen. All my parents think about is this . . . this . . . brain stuff."

"Where are your parents now?"

"They're back in my room."

I wish my mom were just down the hall. I try to push that thought aside.

"I don't think you need to sneak out of the hospital to see places. Your parents are here. Can't you just tell them you want to go and see stuff?"

"Jason D," she says, and I put my finger to my lips, warning her not to say my name out loud.

She nods, and lowers her voice. She still sounds very determined, though. "You don't know what it's like. They don't even want to hear about what I want to do. It's all about what they think we should do. I'm just supposed to go along with everything as if it doesn't bother me. For once, I want to be in charge of me and I just want to be me. Not the girl with the . . . genius issues."

"Max, I really don't want to get you in trouble. They're probably already wondering where you are."

"They're meeting with some doctors now. And I told them I needed some space anyway—to do, you know, typical genius hobbies."

She waves her hand in the air as if I should know what

a typical genius activity is. Or maybe she wants me to ask. I take the bait.

"What's a typical genius hobby?"

"Thinking. Sculpting. Writing. I'm actually writing a book," she says, tapping her finger on the cover of her notebook.

"What kind of book?" I ask. I've never written more than three pages.

"It's an autobiography. The story of my life, so far. There's lots still happening every day, so I'm just trying to keep up with . . . well, myself."

Max is like no one I've ever met. Teaming up with her is either the worst idea ever or the best thing that could happen to me.

"Getting out of here isn't going to be that easy. I think you could use a little help from someone like me. I bring experience, my friend. I know how to trick the docs and nurses."

"What are you talking about?"

"It's not hard. They asked me to pee into a little plastic cup once. I went into the bathroom and poured apple juice into the cup instead. They rushed it off to the lab for some test and came back so panicked that I burst out laughing. Another time, I rubbed some faded blue marker on my fingertips and palms right before a nurse came in to check me. I pretended to be shivering under the covers and showed her my hands. She hooked me up to three different machines before she figured out what I'd done."

This girl might just be a genius after all.

"I've . . . uh . . . noticed that the nurses and docs use a badge to swipe in and out of the locked door," I say, testing the waters.

"I've noticed a few things too," Max adds. She puts her notebook aside and peeks into the hallway to be sure no one's coming in.

We spend the next forty-seven minutes designing our grand escape.

Eleven

At five thirty in the morning, my eyes are closed but I am wide awake. It's still dark outside when Nurse Eric enters.

"Hey, buddy," he whispers. He puts a stethoscope to my chest and swipes a thermometer across my forehead while I pretend to sleep. Eric stands at the curtain inside my room for a moment, silently, as if giving me one last chance to wake and speak. When I don't, he turns and leaves.

A few moments later, my door opens quietly, and Max slips in with a teal backpack at her side. I am sitting upright in my bed and watch her enter. She closes the door behind her and presses her nose to the glass to check once more if anyone's spotted her.

"Did your dad wake up?" I ask in a whisper.

"He didn't even twitch. He's snoring hard on the pull-out chair right now."

I am reassured. Still, we need to move fast.

"Ready to wash your hands?"

First, we head into the bathroom and rub soap and hand lotion onto our wrists. This part was my idea. I saw my mom do this once to get off a ring that was too tight. With a whole lot of wiggling, we're able to take the security bands off. The bandages on Max's hands get wet, and I watch as she takes them off. She tries to turn away but not before I see lots of thin red scratches on the palms of her hands.

"What happened to your hands?" I ask.

"Just a scratch. It's no big deal." I've learned that when people say "no big deal" with that tone of voice, that's a sure sign of a very big deal. We slip the security bracelets into the top drawer of my nightstand.

"So, how'd it happen?"

"How'd it happen? I was . . . I was working on a sculpture. Did I mention I carve sculptures out of wood? Kind of like the ones you see in museums. Cool stuff but lots of splinters."

Carving sculptures, I repeat in my head. My most incredible sculpture was a soccer ball I made out of

Play-Doh when I was four years old. It was not something that belonged in a museum, but my mom kept it on our coffee table for so long that it dried and crumbled. Max and I are two entirely different people, I realize. She's American and has parents who can travel with her and stay in a New York City hotel. That's not my world at all. I'm American but a different kind of American. I don't know how Max and I ended up doing what we're doing together.

We change into the clothes we were wearing when we came into the hospital. For Max, that means jeans and a red-and-white-striped long-sleeved tee. For me, it's jeans and a green polo shirt. We put our sneakers on and lace up. Then we put our hospital gowns on over our clothes just in case anyone pops in before we're ready to make our exit.

I am at the door, peering into the hallway to see if there are any nurses wandering around. The nurses have just finished their last overnight checks, and Max said no other nurses will come in until well after the seven a.m. shift change. Max and I asked for extra snacks last night so we've got a few packets of graham crackers and a few apple juice cups with foil lids as well. She throws the snacks into her backpack.

"Basic survival skills—always think of food."

Max zips the bag, and I cross the room to look out the window. On the street, I see a fruit vendor stacking oranges and small plastic containers of strawberries on his cart. The sidewalks, the buildings, the lights—they all seem to sparkle with excitement. People call New York "the city that never sleeps," but I think it must close its eyes at some point. How else could it rise and shine with the energy I can feel buzzing from the sidewalks and into the hospital's walls before the sun is even up?

"It's almost time," I say, taking a deep breath.

"Nervous?" Max asks me.

"Can't be," I say simply. It's the truth. There's no room for nerves. I need to find Auntie Seema, the only person who really knows me, and the only person who could possibly help me reconnect with my mom.

Max is rolling her shoulders, as if she's getting ready to pitch a ball.

"I saw Eric sitting at the desk on my way over here."

"Sitting there? Then he's going to see us!"

"Would you relax? That's what he's done for the past two days. I can't sleep well in hospitals, so I've been watching him."

I close my eyes for a beat. Just because I can't be nervous doesn't mean I'm not. I might sneak onto rooftops to feed pigeons, but I'm not the kind of kid who breaks big rules. This is all new to me.

"All right, let's look then. It's almost time."

Max opens the door. I'm right behind her, looking to see if Eric's still sitting at the nurses' desk. He's not. Max silently points out a sweatshirt hanging on the back of a rolling chair. There's an ID badge clipped to the open zipper.

"Easy grab," Max whispers.

"Close the door," I reply, and Max does. She turns around and looks at me. It's time for the next phase of our escape plan. "Ready to play hair stylist?"

I nod and Max pulls a pair of wide-bladed scissors out of her backpack—the kind nurses use to cut gauze and tape. She sits sideways on the edge of the hospital bed. I start clipping the wires as close to her scalp as possible. The rainbow-colored wires fall away, and Max is left with her straight brown hair. Her fingers start scratching at her scalp where clumps of glue hold stickers in place. She pulls a baseball cap out of her backpack and puts it on. It's got a picture of a woman in a blue-collared shirt showing off her bicep muscle. Her hair's tied back in a red bandanna, and she's got a no-nonsense look on her face. It's the perfect hat for Max, and it hides the frayed ends of the wires I've trimmed.

Cutting the wires means we are definitely going through with this plan. How could we explain what happened to her wires? We turn our attention back to getting off this pediatric floor. Locked double doors stand between us and the elevator bank, which is why we need Eric's ID. If we swipe his card at the door's security panel, the doors will swing open and get us closer to the outside world. Since our security bracelets are off, we won't set off any alarms once we're on the other side.

I open the door again. I am nervous, but the clock is ticking. As we get closer to seven o'clock, the day shift nurses will start trickling in, and there'll be more of a chance of us being spotted. We slip out of our hospital gowns and quietly duck into the hallway, the backpack strapped onto Max's shoulders. The fluorescent hospital lights are still dimmed, and it's so quiet that I can hear my heart thumping in my ears. If anyone spots us now, we're doomed. There's no way to explain our street clothes, Max's wireless head, or why our security bands are in a drawer instead of on our wrists.

Max hunches forward and tiptoes over to the half-circle work station where all the computers and chairs are clustered. With the grace of a ninja, she slides through the opening and crouches under the counter. I can see just the top of her hat bobbing as she inches her way to the chair with Eric's sweatshirt.

I'm pressed against the door of another room. My job is to be the lookout and warn Max if I see anyone. I can hear voices coming from behind the door of the staff room, just behind the work area. The sound of beeping monitors and the hum of a breathing treatment make it impossible to listen for footsteps.

Between computer screens, I see Max's hand reach toward the sweatshirt. Her fingers blindly grab at the zipper. She's trying to stay under the counter and maintain her cover, but her hand is making the chair swivel and roll around, and the ID badge goes farther out of reach.

I am about to whisper to Max to just stand up, grab the badge, and go when I hear the double doors down the hall swing open. I hear the rattle of wheels.

Someone's coming.

My room is too far down the hallway to make it back there. Max pokes her head out from under the desk. She's heard the wheels too. The light of the computer screen gives her face an eerie glow. We lock eyes and understand that we've both got to hide. Without thinking, I open the door behind me and disappear into a patient room. I am relieved to see an empty bed and turn back to look through the glass window in the middle of the door. I peek out nervously, certain I'm going to watch Max get caught where she has no business being. If she gets in trouble, it's going to be all my fault.

A man comes down the hallway. With one hand, he's

pushing a beige cart with narrow drawers. As he walks, he's reading from a piece of paper he holds with his other hand.

Max is so startled that she goes from a sneaky ninja to a lumbering bear. I hear a grunt and then see the empty chair roll from one side of the half circle to the other, and the man freezes, his eyes turning to the center of the main nursing station and widening. Behind the counter, the chair comes to a slow stop but continues to spin, spookily.

The man blinks slowly and looks around as if he's hoping someone will confirm what he's just witnessed. He adjusts the thick, round lenses on his face and scratches at his cheek. He leaves the cart and makes his way to the counter. My breath catches in my chest to see him getting closer and closer to where Max is cowering.

The man stands just inches away from Max, separated only by a thin piece of plywood beneath the desk. The man stares at the chair, now motionless, and takes one final look around. He looks like he's been up all night.

By some small miracle, he does not detect the ninja under the counter. He also does not spot the wide-eyed boy staring at him through the square of glass. He rubs his eyes with his fingertips and goes back to rolling his cart down the hallway.

I slip back into the hall just as Max emerges from beneath the counter. There's the sound of another door opening and closing, somewhere down the opposite end of the hall, in the direction of both our rooms. In a flash, Max is beside me, pulling me toward the double doors and away from the fast-approaching footsteps. In front of us, just a few yards down the dimly lit hallway, I see the locked doors and my stomach sinks, thinking of the way Eric's sweatshirt rolled away from Max. Without that ID badge, we're running toward a brick wall.

"Max, the locks—"

"Come on!"

In one swift motion, she pulls Eric's ID out of her back pocket and swipes it against the security panel on the wall. The doors spread open like bird's wings, and Max and I bolt through them, uncaged.

Max hits the button for the elevator, and we look back at the closed double doors. We're both expecting someone to burst through them. That's when I spy the door to the stairwell.

"This way!" I say, and put my weight behind the door to swing it open.

"Good idea," Max says. Her voice sounds shaky but I can't tell if she's nervous or excited. The stairwell is empty, and we go down the steps as quickly as we can. I can hear the tinny echo of her feet and mine as we land on each step. Down nine flights of stairs we go. When we reach the ground floor, I shoot Max a look of caution.

"Max . . ."

I'm giving her one last chance to turn back.

"You're not going to survive out there without me," she says.

"But your parents are going to flip out, Max. You don't have to do this."

Max puts one hand on the metal lever of the door. She looks at me, unblinking.

"Jason D, this is my only chance," she says. With one push she swings the door open and propels us into the stirring city street.

Twelve

"Do you always smile like that?" Max mutters out of the corner of her mouth.

"Like what?"

"Like you're sitting in the dentist's chair?"

My lips clamp shut. I didn't think my smile was that wide.

"I don't want people to think we've done something wrong," I explain.

"Then I'd suggest getting that suspicious grin off your face."

Max and I are on the sidewalk, sneakers hitting the concrete with a steady rhythm. We're walking fast enough to give people the impression we know where we're going.

It's now 7:20. The sun will be up in a few minutes.

The nurses will be huddling by the computers, coffee mugs in hand, for change of shift. Any minute now, someone will walk into my room and gasp to see an empty bed and severed wires. Down the hall, another nurse will be waking Max's snoring father to ask him where she's gone.

I look at the people walking toward us. Their eyes are trained straight ahead or on the ground. I don't look directly at them. Instead, I spy their reflections as I look into the window displays of the shops and restaurants. Max catches me investigating and nods approvingly.

"How much farther to the subway?"

"It's a few more blocks," Max answers. "I remember seeing the entrance on my way into the hospital. Maybe we should ask someone."

"We can't ask anyone, Max. The police are already on my case, and soon people are going to be looking for both of us. The more people we talk to, the more likely it is we're going to get caught. We're going to have to figure it out."

We see a man coming toward us, less than a block away. He's walking two dogs, their leashes crossing and uncrossing as the dogs try to get ahead of each other. One is a wolf-like, white German shepherd, and the other is a much smaller mixed breed. The man's wearing warm-up pants and a white T-shirt with *Brooklyn* written across the chest. He's looking at us with a curious expression. He slows his step, and it's easy to see the dogs aren't too happy about it. Their leashes are stretched taut, and they turn their heads to see what's holding their owner back.

"Should we cross the street?" Max asks.

I think of the mess under her hat. Then I wonder how it'll look if we suddenly dart across the street midblock. This is followed closely by the memory of my mother telling me crossing the street anywhere but the crosswalk is a crime called jaywalking.

"Let's just play it cool. Maybe he's not looking at us."

That's wishful thinking. While it is New York City, the sidewalks are far less crowded then they would normally be because:

It's just around sunrise.

It's a Sunday.

The man's squinting and his lips are parted, ready to shape words. Max stops abruptly. She beats him to the punch and starts talking.

"Excuse me, sir?" she says sweetly.

I gasp. Until this very moment, I never thought it was possible to choke on air.

"Everything okay, kids?" The man's eyes scan the sidewalk as if to find an adult to assign us to.

95

"Everything's fine with us. And how are you today?" Max sounds deeply concerned—about him. For someone who called my smile suspicious, she's being awfully cheery.

"Uh . . . great, thanks for asking," the man replies with a chuckle. "What are you kids up to so early?"

I'm sweating. There's a glob of paste poking out from Max's cap. I wonder if this guy's noticed it.

"Just trying to change the world, sir."

"Change the . . ." The man looks as stumped as I feel.

"Yes, sir. My friend and I want to change the world," Max says, waving her hand in my direction with the flair of a magician. "We're out trying to raise money so that we can open a children's center. Anything you'd be willing to donate would be greatly appreciated."

"What kind of children's center?" he asks, giving a gentle tug on the German shepherd's leash. The dog has started to lick my hand. I let him, praying he has no K-9 dog cousins who have taught him to sniff out people running from the law.

"It's going to be called Gamers' Galaxy. We're going to have all kinds of video games for kids to play. It'll be free for boys and girls. We're going to offer snacks and special tips to help the youth sharpen their skills on games like . . ." There's a slight pause in Max's speech but then it picks up with the upbeat tone of a brilliant idea. "Max Attacks."

I can't believe my ears. She's either a genius or trying to give us away.

The man shakes his head and stares at Max as if he's not believing her completely. "I've never heard of . . ."

I can't let this fall apart. My mouth opens and I follow Max's lead.

"I'm surprised you haven't. Max Attacks has seventeen different levels, and you can only move from one to the next if you kidnap the king and take over his minions."

Max jumps back in.

"Did you happen to see that Gavin Hopewell movie with the robots? It's based on that movie. Man, he was an unstoppable warrior in that movie and this game is just like . . . like—" she says, looking for the right words to describe the character.

"Right, right. Listen, where are your parents? Is someone here with you?"

Max slips her backpack off her shoulders and gives a quick nod to the store we're standing in front of.

"Yup, my mom's just printing up some more donation forms in her office on the second floor. She's got a little credit card gadget too so we can take cards if you don't have the cash. I've got a form right here," she says as she starts to unzip her book bag.

"Oh, is that so? You know what, I'd love to help but forgot my wallet at home this morning," he says with a disappointed shrug. He drops the leash a bit and the smaller dog lets out a yelp as he pulls forward. "Good luck, though."

He's gone, both he and the dogs looking relieved to be on their way. I look at Max and burst out laughing.

"I can't believe you just did that!"

"I can't believe *you* just did that!" Max grins and starts walking again. We walk another three blocks, then she pauses at the corner and looks left and right. She adjusts her cap and smooths her hair behind her ears.

"C'mon. I think it's another block over."

"I thought you said it was—"

"It's gotta be close. We walked out of the subway station and then we were at the hospital in a couple of minutes."

She steps off the curb and into the street when I pull her back with a tug on her backpack.

"Max, we might be walking in the wrong direction."

Max looks flustered. She squints against the morning sun. She doesn't look as confident as she did when we talked this over in the hospital.

"We probably just missed it by a block."

I let out a slow breath. Max has no idea which way we should go.

"Max, I think we should try a different direction."

Max is speed-walking now, her thumbs hooked under the backpack straps on her chest. I jog a few steps to catch up with her. Her jaw is clenched tight.

"Max! Hey, just listen for a second!"

A flush of red is rising from her neck to her cheeks. Her eyes glisten in the sun.

"Max. It's all right. We'll find the subway station. We can do this, okay?"

Max stops abruptly and presses her hands against her head.

"I just need to think."

I don't know what to say. This is the first time I've seen Max look anything but cool and collected.

"Let's sit here for a minute," I say, and lead her to a bus shelter. The metal bench feels cool even through my jeans. I rub my hands together. Outside the bus shelter is a sign with letters and numbers. My riddle-solving skills can't figure out what the numbers and letters mean.

"Max, we can figure it out together." Max is getting more frustrated. Maybe she's realizing this was a big mistake. She thinks her parents don't care much about her, but I can't imagine that to be true. She's got American parents and probably lives in a nice house. She's smart and funny. Unlike me, she doesn't have any real problems.

"Max, you don't have to do this," I say quietly. "I can walk you back to the hospital and then try to get to Seventy-Fourth Street on my own."

Max looks hurt that I would make such a suggestion,

but she doesn't say anything. Maybe she's considering it.

"Aren't you scared to be on your own, Jason D?"

Of course I am. But I don't have a choice right now. I've been alone since those two men put my mom in their car. I've heard people on television talking about what should happen to undocumented people, but I never thought they were talking about my mother.

"I am."

Her face looks a little strange to me. She's staring off like she can see something I can't. Her lips are twitching. I'm a little worried but I don't know what to do. After a few seconds, she gets up and walks out of the bus shelter. I follow her.

"Max?"

"I remember now," she says with both hands on her temples. "I see it. This city is shaped like a banana. The avenues run from top to bottom. The streets are shorter and they go across." She looks at the street sign on the corner and then strains to see the sign on the next block. I follow her, catching on to how this works.

"That means Seventy-Fourth Street is going to be that way. We can just keep walking."

"It's a really long walk," Max says. She's dropped her hands to her sides again and takes a seat at the bus shelter. "I have a T-shirt at home with the New York City subway map on it. My mom got it for me when I told her I wanted to see stuff in the city. She gave me that T-shirt and a small Statue of Liberty figure, as if that was close enough to the real thing. We need to find the subway. Walking the whole way will take forever."

We start moving up the avenue again, street numbers climbing, which means we're going in the right direction.

"We never come into the city," I tell Max. "My mom's always been really scared of it because she's always hearing about something bad happening here. She was afraid it would be too much like Afghanistan. I guess some stuff is hard to forget."

"For me, lots of stuff is hard to forget." Max has her eyes on the concrete as we walk.

"Like Gavin Hopewell's movies?" I like him too. I like having things in common with Max. She's a real American, the kind who never gets asked where she's from. Everything would be different if I were more like her.

"Who could forget his movies? Even the one about the baseball team was good," she says with a small smile. "No, I'm talking about remembering weird things."

"What do you mean?"

"Like sometimes I remember being in a place, but I've never been there before. Sometimes I remember stuff that my parents forget, but I can see it in my head like a scene from a movie. Like once, I remembered what my grandfather was wearing the last Christmas we had with him before he died. It's like having a treasure box that sometimes opens and out pops something shiny and cool."

"Is that part of the whole genius thing?"

Max blinks twice and kicks away a chunk of concrete that's come loose off the sidewalk.

"I guess so." Max doesn't sound as cheerful about it as she should.

A car honks as it passes us, and I see Max jump and pick up her pace. She's avoiding my eyes. Everything about her tells me she's running away from something more than overbearing parents. I can spot a puzzle when I see one, and it's clear to me that this girl with her treasure box of memories doesn't want to be figured out.

Thirteen

Just beneath New York City's surface lies a network of subway tracks. It's like an ant farm with a world of movement hidden underground. Max tells me what the subway station looks like. As we walk, my eyes stay peeled for a black subway sign on green railings. It's now eight thirty and we still haven't found what we're looking for.

I gulp when I spy two police cars coming down the cross street.

"Jason D . . ."

Max has seen the cars too.

"Red door on your left," I say sharply, and she follows me up the three concrete steps to the doors. I wish I had eyeballs on the back of my head so I could see if we're being followed.

The door is heavy but between the two of us, we are able to pull it open wide enough to slip through. We stand with our backs to the door for a second. We've entered a dimly lit room that is long and deep. At the far end is a podium with an explosion of color behind it. The glass wall looks something like a kaleidoscope. On either side of a center aisle, there are rows and rows of empty wooden benches.

For a second I think this is some kind of theater. Then I spot a cross on the wall and I realize we're standing in a church. To my left, there's a pedestal filled with sand. A colony of thin candles stands in the sand, a few of them flickering with yellow flames. Some have melted into pools of wax.

There are a few people sitting on the benches. Max points toward them and motions me forward.

"Let's go sit in case the police come in here. They won't recognize the backs of our heads," she whispers.

I've never sat in a church before so I follow Max's lead. She slides into the center of an empty row, but it's the third bench from the front of the church. We keep our heads low and hear the people around us talking quietly. Some have come alone, some have come as a family. We take a few moments to catch our breath.

"Maybe we can slip back out now," I suggest. But just as I say the words, light spills into the room and a flood of people enter through the heavy doors behind us. Max and I look at each other as people fill the seats on either side of us, locking us in.

"If this Sunday service is anything like the one I go to, we'll be here for an hour. Should we . . ." Max whispers.

"Everyone will look at us," I warn.

And so we sit through a service. A priest stands at the podium and thanks everyone for coming. I listen and learn a few things. The people in this church pray with hands clasped together. My mom and I pray with our hands cupped. They say Amen. We say *Ameen*. They believe God is kind. So do we.

I think of the candles I saw when we first entered. The candles remind me of the day every year when my mother goes a little quieter than usual. Once a year, in late November, she makes *maleeda*, a bowl of finely crumbled cake that looks something like graham cracker crumbs. It is the only time she talks about my father. She puts his framed picture on the table and plants birthday candles in the mound of *maleeda*. Sugar crystals sparkle under the orange glow of the flame. My mom and I sit at the kitchen table and close our eyes. We cup our hands together and she recites a quiet prayer, words I don't understand, but the sounds give me comfort because I've heard them so many times. My mother always sighs as if she's sort of relieved after she says them.

Every year, she shares something new with me. Over the years, I've learned that my father loved spicy food and folk music. At weddings, he danced with his arms spread wide like he was going to embrace the whole party. When he was seven years old, he rode his bike into a ditch and broke a rib. He was a terrible singer, but that never stopped him from trying. He loved words and had a small collection of his most favorite books.

I always want my mother to tell me more, but she shakes her head each time.

It's hard to talk about, my little king.

"Jason." Max pulls at my arm. People have started to stand and file out of the church. We follow and make our way to the doors.

"It's nine thirty," I say, catching a glimpse of the screen of a cell phone. "We just need to stay hidden in crowds. We stick out too much on these streets."

"I did an essay on the subway system for my social studies class in our modern transportation unit. The New York City subway has over two hundred miles of train routes and millions of daily riders," she says with authority. "It should be pretty hard to find two kids in tunnels that move millions of people. The sooner we get to the subway station, the better."

We stand on the steps of the church for a moment and, confirming that the coast is clear, make our way back to the sidewalk. We walk another few blocks and pass a photocopy shop, a shoe store, four nail salons, a Chinese restaurant, and two Mexican restaurants. It's like they've taken my entire town of Elkton and squeezed it into a couple of streets.

We go two blocks up, looking both ways at the cross-walk to spot a subway entrance. There are people walking in all directions around us, but most certainly not a million of them.

"How can it be this hard to find millions of people? Ugh!" Max's frustration is boiling over. She looks at her watch.

A police car stops at the intersection one block away. It's at a red light, and I can see an elbow resting on the rolled-down window. Is that one of the two cars that passed by us earlier? I feel my palms grow moist and rub them on my pants.

Don't get nervous, I tell myself.

"Hey, Max. Do you smell that?"

The light turns green but the police car doesn't move. Instead, it pulls over to the curb. Because of the sun's glare and the distance, it's impossible to tell if the driver is looking at us.

"We've got bigger problems than funky smells, in case you haven't noticed," Max says through gritted teeth.

I feel steam rising from beneath me. It smells faintly like metal and old trash. I look down and realize I'm standing on a grate. I tug at Max's elbow as I feel a rumbling giant pass beneath us.

"Max, that's the train! It's right under us!"

If the train is under us, there must be an entrance nearby. We look around and spot it. Just a few feet before the parked police car is the subway entrance, marked with two tall green lamps and a black placard with the numbers four and six in green circles. Glancing up every few seconds, we speed walk to the end of the block. I wonder if the officer is watching us or calling in backup.

The car door opens and a uniformed policeman steps out, adjusting his sunglasses. He's talking into a phone that's pressed to his ear.

It can't be a coincidence that we've seen three police cars in less than an hour.

I feel a rush of air rising up from the stairwell, and the ground vibrates beneath my feet. Two hundred miles of train routes, four hundred stations, and millions of people of camouflage—this is our best chance at avoiding capture.

"Max, stick close!"

Max is as ready for this moment as I am. We hurry down the steps, pressed against the handrail with heads lowered. The people coming out of the station move like a swarm of bees and bump against us as they climb the stairs. There's the garbled sound of an announcement in the background.

When we get down to the station, I spot a turnstile and two ticket machines. They look similar to the ones at the train station in Elkton but different colors. Max takes out a ten-dollar bill.

"My mom's always nagging me to spend my allowance on something useful," she says with a mischievous smile.

I tap on the screen to purchase a subway card. Max slides the money into the slot, and the machine clinks and hums before it spits out a yellow card.

Max is on my heels as I swipe the card through the slot, and a green light gives a go sign. I press my torso against the metal bar and hand the card back to her so she can follow. We walk onto the platform. The last few people are getting off a train marked with a green four on the outside. We step into the emptied train car, and I slide into a seat.

"Hey, Max."

"Yup." Max has taken a seat beside me and placed her backpack on her lap. She cracks open her notebook just wide enough so that she can read and I can't. The doors are still open and the train hasn't started moving yet.

"I'm going to pay you back for this."

"Whatever." She shrugs off my promise. I think back to how flustered she looked earlier, and know that today might not work out the way we want it to. I want to see her smile again.

"I *will* make it up to you. And if we end up back in the hospital, I'll give you all my meal trays."

"That's awful, Jason D," Max groans. She leans her head back and smiles briefly. "I'm pretty sure this train's going in the right direction, but I wish we could ask someone to be sure."

No one else has entered this car of the train, which is odd. I wonder if Max's research is completely off, or if the passengers have all boarded the other train cars. Then I see it, a framed poster between two windows.

"Max, I have rivers without water, forests without trees, mountains without rocks, and towns without houses. What am I?"

Her eyes look off into the corner as she thinks.

"I dunno. What are you?"

"A map, Max," I say as I walk over to the poster on the opposite side of the train. "A map."

The poster is a map of the entire subway system with dots naming each of the stations on different-colored lines.

"Here," I say, pointing to the station. The sign outside said we were on Thirty-Third Street. "If we take this train up, it'll stop at Seventy-Seventh Street. That's just three blocks away from my aunt's apartment."

"And the zoo is by Sixty-Fourth Street," Max adds. "My parents are staying in a hotel close by. That's right on the way there. We're so close, Jason D! Maybe we can go to the zoo and then you go to your aunt's house and I'll go back to the hospital before anyone even realizes I'm gone."

Seeing those crisscrossing lines and black dots makes me feel like I'll make it to my aunt's home. There are steps we can follow. The path is clear. We sit back down in the hard seats, feeling like our plan is coming together.

A long growl comes from Max's stomach. She wraps her arms around her belly.

"I'm hungry too," I admit.

"Let's eat, then." Max unzips her backpack and pulls out a couple of graham cracker packets and two juice containers. The apple juice is too sweet, but we need to wash down the dry graham crackers. I lean back and close my eyes, praying the train will start moving and amazed at how far Max and I have come this morning.

"Hey, you two!"

My eyelids fly open and the sweet taste in my mouth turns sour. There's a man standing in the open doors of the train, his hands on his hips and his face stern. He's wearing a navy-blue uniform with some kind of official patch on the arm, and his cap has a gold shield on it. I see a walkie-talkie hooked on his belt.

There's a buzzing in my ear, and I look at Max.

"Oh no." Max breathes those two faint words, her shoulders rising and falling. Gone is the confidence she had when we were stopped by the man with his dogs. She's not in any shape to talk us out of this situation.

The man beckons us to follow him with one crooked finger. I bury my face in my hands. Just when I thought we were getting somewhere!

A few subway stops from freedom, we've been caught.

Fourteen

"What do you kids think you're doing?"

I don't want to answer that question, and, judging by how silent she is, neither does Max.

"I'm asking you a question. Can't either of you talk?"

I slide back into the seat and groan. I've had about all I can take. I'm too tired to try to wiggle my way out of this. I've been doing my best to be brave since I saw my mom being taken away, but the truth is being brave is hard. I'm exhausted. Why was I too scared to jump into that car with my mom? At least now I'd be with her instead of on the run.

No more, I think. *I don't know how you did it for so long, Madar. I've only been at this for a day and I'm falling apart.*

I've lied to the doctors and nurses who were trying to help me. Even worse, I've dragged Max into this mess too. The lump on my head throbs with regret.

"Fine!" I blurt out as I stand up. "Go ahead and lock me up or throw me into a home."

"Uh, Jason . . ." Max tugs at the hem of my shirt.

"No," I insist. "I'm done. It's over."

"Jason, you may want to shut your mouth for a second," Max hisses. Her eyes are burning into me, but I've got to put an end to this.

"No, I'm ready for this. Where are the handcuffs? Let's just get it over with."

The man lets out a low whistle.

"Man, why don't you save the theatrics for Broadway," the man snaps. He's shaking his head. "Sheesh! And on a Sunday morning? I'm already dealing with a stalled train, and now I've got to talk Billy the Kid here off the ledge? No way. This is not what I signed up for."

"Billy the who? I'm not—"

"Whatever you're going to say, save it. You were probably babbling when the announcement went on too. This train is out of service, kids. Now get up and get out before I call the cops!"

The cops? I look at the badge on the man's cap and feel confused. Max is on her feet and sliding the straps of her backpack over her shoulders.

"Always gotta be Mr. Funny Guy, right?" Max says through a tight smile. "Please stop messing with the nice *train conductor* and let's go."

Train conductor? Oh no.

I bite my tongue.

"Man, kids today want to turn everything into some big protest." The conductor is walking away from us now, shaking his head and muttering to himself as he plods through the empty train car. "'Lock me up,' he tells me. Man, when I was that age I never would've . . ."

His words drift off as he opens the door at the far end of the car and steps from this train car into the next. The metal door slides shut behind him.

Max jabs at my chest with one daggerlike finger.

"You almost did us in, Jason D!"

Why hadn't I paid more attention to his uniform? It's just starting to hit me how close I came to sabotaging our mission. I'm not going to get anywhere if I'm that ready to call it quits.

"Let's get out of here before he comes back," I say, finally able to breathe again. Max and I take the steps two at a time until we're out of the station and back on the sidewalk. Luckily, the police car is gone.

"Come on, let's get moving before that guy decides to call someone who will throw me in jail."

We start walking, looking over our shoulders every few

minutes and trying to put as much distance between us and the train conductor as possible.

"I'm so hungry," Max groans. I am too but I try not to think about it.

"Let's get a little farther and then we'll find something to eat."

Max nods her head in agreement. We are walking steadily, trying not to draw attention from any of the people around us. When we get to the end of the block, I look both ways and start to cross. Max pulls at my elbow.

"Uh, Jason . . ." she says.

I follow her gaze and look up at a green sign on the corner.

"Oh no."

The sign says First Avenue. We've walked across the island instead of up! I cover my face with my hands.

"I think we're both hungry. We better eat something before we make another big mistake," Max says with a pained expression. "And if I don't eat something soon, you're going to have to pick me up and carry me."

"We're all out of juice and crackers," I report, but Max already knows that. "We'll find something soon. Try not to think about it." Wanting to get her mind off her stomach, I remember a brain teaser game my teacher used to play with us. "Answer this. Twelve *M* in a *Y*. What's the *M* and what's the *Y*?"

"What are you talking about?"

"Twelve Months in a Year," I explain. "Get it? I'll give you some more. You have to fill in the blanks. Fifty-two *C* in a *D*."

"I'm too hungry to think," Max says with a scowl. We continue walking. The street signs tell us we're actually headed uptown, which is a relief. After a moment, I hear my friend mutter something under her breath.

"Fifty-two Cards in a Deck."

Once she gets one, she wants more, because it feels good to solve a puzzle. I know the feeling.

Sixteen *O* in a *P*. Five *D* in a *ZC*. Three hundred sixty-six *D* in an *LY*.

Sixteen Ounces in a Pound. Five Digits in a Zip Code. Three hundred sixty-six Days in a Leap Year.

"Hey, what does the *D* stand for?" Max asks.

"Which *D*?"

"In your name. Jason D. What does the *D* stand for?"

"Oh, that *D*." I've never told anyone the story, mostly because I think it sounds weird that my mother came up with name by staring at a calendar.

"It's a weird story."

"Meaning it's perfect for today."

I grin.

"It stands for *December*."

"December? That's a strange middle name."

"My mother wanted to give me an American name, so she chose Jason. When I was born, one of the nurses asked if she wanted to pick a middle name. She thought if I at least had a middle initial, maybe I'd seem more American. Then she looked at the calendar. July, August, September, October, November . . ."

"That is so cool."

There it is again—that feeling that I'm a little more normal if Max says so.

After a couple of blocks, the number of people on the sidewalk has swelled. It's starting to feel as if the crowd will absorb us and move us.

"Jason D, look! Let's stop there." We're on Fifty-Seventh Street and definitely due for a break.

Max is pointing to a small grocery store with fruit displays out front. We cross at the light and walk through pyramids of oranges, apples, and kiwis. There's also an open ice-filled cooler with bottled water and juices. The store is not very deep but has a few racks filled with packaged foods and a case holding premade sandwiches that make my mouth water. An older woman stands behind the cash register, ringing up customers and snapping paper bags open to stuff them with purchases. Max pulls out another ten-dollar bill and uses it to pay for a sandwich and bottle of cranberry juice.

I walk outside while she waits for her change. When

she comes out, she pulls out the sandwich and gives me half. It feels good to eat something other than hospital food. We take a seat at the small table set up on the sidewalk and eat.

"My genius powers are recharging," Max declares as she brushes the crumbs from her lap.

We've made it about two blocks when the sidewalk traffic thickens even more. There are people everywhere. A few people are holding up cardboard signs with photographs or messages on them. We're bumping shoulder to shoulder just like we were when we went into the subway station.

"Is it always this crazy here?" I ask Max, but she can't hear me because two guys behind us just started yelling.

"NYPD runners!"

NYPD stands for New York Police Department. I remember seeing those blue block letters on the side of the patrol car. I spy a couple of police officers standing in the street, right by the curb. They look like they're scanning the flood of faces passing by them.

There's chanting around us.

"Car-ter! Car-ter! Car-ter! After the twenty-six point two, we'll be waiting here for you!"

Two girls much older than us are standing nearby. They're snapping pictures of the crowd with their cell phones raised high over their heads.

"Hey, um, what's all this about?" I lean over and ask, my voice a shout.

They both give me puzzled looks. One girl, wearing a pale-green windbreaker, tilts her head to the side.

"What's what about?"

"All this," I say, pointing at the crowd. "Is there something happening today?"

"You're pranking me," she says with eyes bright as headlights. "A jokester, huh?"

I wasn't trying to be.

Her friend laughs. "'Is something happening?' That's hilarious!"

"Had ya for a second, didn't I?" I smile broadly and shrug before I turn back to Max in defeat. The girls shuffle forward and move a few yards ahead of us. I notice a man with *26.2* printed on the back of his long-sleeved shirt.

"We've got problems," Max yells.

"You think?" My reply comes out slightly sarcastic but it's too loud for Max to notice.

"My mom called. She's—how can I put this? Do you remember the T. rex in *Jurassic Park*? She makes him look serene. She's that kind of angry."

"How did your mom call?"

Max holds up a flip phone. She gives her best mysterious look, eyes mostly closed and mouth a thin, serious line. She's much calmer now that we've had the sandwich.

"You have a phone," I say with surprise.

"Yeah, she's really anxious about us staying in touch. It would be cool if this phone did something besides make calls and take pictures. I'm pretty sure dinosaurs used more advanced technology."

"What did you tell your mom?"

"I told her that I'm fine and that I'll be back, but I have something to do first. She's flipping out, of course, and crazy mad at my dad for sleeping through our exit. She was begging me to tell her where we are."

Max holds a red button and I see the phone power down.

"We?"

"Oh, yeah. The nurses realized we'd run off together. I got off the line quickly. You have to, otherwise they trace the call. Criminals always get caught like that on TV. She says they locked down the whole hospital looking for us. They thought we were still in the building. How cool is that?"

My heart thumps in my chest. I want to hide. I want to be tucked under my mother's arm. I want to be small, but this is getting bigger and bigger with every passing minute.

I can hardly hear myself think over the cheering.

"Lookin' good, runner!"

"Way to move!"

We're pressed up against the back of a blue banner, a barricade between us and the street. Like the flash of a camera going off in my head, the number 26.2 comes alive with meaning.

26.2 M in an M.

Max and I are on the sidelines of the New York City Marathon—a race that's twenty-six point two miles long.

Fifteen

"*I* guess the millions of people have decided to run today instead of taking the subway."

Max has read my mind.

We stare at the cloud of runners, sneakers hitting the cracked asphalt of the city street with a steady rhythm. It's a swarm of spandex pants, water bottles fixed to sports belts, and numbered bibs. Some runners smile or wave as they go by. Others keep their eyes trained straight ahead.

I know what my mom would say if she could see this.

So many people running because they want to—so many run because they have to.

The streets are clogged with spectators. Everyone is aboveground today. The police officers, I realize now, are here for crowd control. They aren't looking at us. They're looking at everyone. There are a couple of officers in the street and more standing behind the spectators. We're sandwiched between them, and that's not exactly a recipe for escape.

The runners are moving in the direction we should be going.

We're now at Sixty-First Street and still three blocks away from the zoo. If we try to backtrack and put distance between us and the crowd, we'll stand out like neon lights in a dark room, and the cops already have their eyes peeled. I'm careful not to look any of them in the eye, afraid that I'll be finding myself staring at Officer Khan. I wouldn't be able to sneak my way out of a run-in with him—not after our last encounter.

"Hey, Max, how do you think we should—"

But my question's left hanging when I turn around and see Max leaning over the banner into the street. She looks like a turtle, her head poking out of her purple shell. She's got both hands cupped around her mouth like a megaphone.

"Pound that pavement, people!"

"Max!"

"It's a marathon, not a crawlathon!" She pulls out her phone again.

I grab her by the book bag and yank her back into the

cover of the crowd. She's got her cell phone in her hand. It's turned on again, and she snaps a photo of the runners before she puts it away.

"What do you think you're doing?"

"I'm cheering on these fine athletes—that's what I'm doing! I'm demonstrating good sportsmanship. You should try it."

"Seriously, Max? Do you not see the cops around here?"

One of the cops swivels his head in our direction as if I'd called him by name. I pull Max deeper into the crowd, back into the folds of people cheering. I duck my head and hold on to my friend's arm, afraid she'll be spotted.

"You're going to have everyone staring at us!"

"I've never seen the New York City Marathon!" Max says sharply. She looks annoyed, as if I've pulled her away from her own birthday party. "I just want to see it! Is that too much to ask?"

I let go of her arm. The crowd around us goes right on cheering despite the fact that two runaway kids are starting to fall apart.

"Max?"

Max's eyes look sad. She's staring at her sneakers as she tells me. I have to lean in to hear her against the yelling.

"My parents keep me away from crowds and noise. They treat me like a delicate little flower, which I'm most definitely not."

The cheering around us falls away and all I hear is Max.

"Can't travel because we'd be too far from my doctors. Can't go to a basketball game because of the lights. Can't do sleepovers. Can't. Can't. Can't."

I pause, trying to imagine what it must be like to live in Max's world. As far as I can see, she's got everything. She doesn't seem to think so. I see flakes of glue in Max's hair and wonder what I'm missing. Why can't she be too far from her doctors?

"Max, why can't you travel too far from your doctors?"

Max inhales sharply.

"I didn't say doctors."

I blink twice. It's loud here but I'm sure I heard her say *doctors*.

"I just heard you say—"

"Jason D," Max says after she takes a deep breath and looks at me through softened eyes. "I'm not some career criminal. This isn't my usual Sunday outing. I'm just trying to get a few good hours in before—"

The hollering gets louder. There's another cluster of runners, faces flushed in this warmer-than-usual weather, coming up the avenue. Everyone's eyes are on the runners, searching out friends or family members who have made it this far in the race. Max turns her attention back to the race, and I can see freedom in her eyes. Whatever it is she's running from, it's more than just some genius testing.

"There are so many people here," I say as I lean toward her ear. "I don't think anyone will even notice us. Let's just watch for a few minutes."

"Seriously?"

I nod. "You know, I wouldn't have gotten this far without you."

Max looks like she might hug me but instead she points a finger at me. The sadness in her eyes has been replaced by the glimmer of mischief.

"That's for sure. Without my badge-swiping skills, you'd be hiding from the police under your hospital bed."

"Max."

"Yeah?"

"I promise to write to you while you're in prison."

"Very funny, Jason D," Max says drily, but her face is beaming with pride. "Very funny."

Bodies of all different colors, shapes, and ages are running. The stream of people continues as far as my eyes can see. The rhythmic swing of their arms and legs is hypnotizing as they float by. Long-sleeved tees and green paper cups lie crumpled on the side of the running path.

Max and I lean farther over the barrier and wave at the runners approaching, their knees and elbows pumping like the parts of an engine. People jog in our neighborhood, sometimes two together, but they never draw a crowd. What is it about this race that makes everyone want to drop what they're doing and watch?

But I'm not as interested as Max. I'm wondering if my mother's found a way to call her best friend yet and if I'll ever hear her voice again.

"Jason D—"

"Yeah?"

"Jay, I think—"

The people around us start cheering louder again. It's like everyone's got a best friend or brother in the pool of runners.

"Jason D!"

Just as Max shouts my name, her voice thick with worry, I lock eyes with a runner whose face I recognize.

Oh no, I think, and my heart starts to pound.

Just when I was starting to feel like we were invisible in this teeming city, I realize how wrong I am.

Sixteen

Max yanks me by the arm, and we disappear into the folds of people and their poster boards.

"Did you just see—"

By the way Max is ducking and squeezing through the crowd, I can tell that she saw Dr. Shabani. I almost didn't recognize her at first. She isn't wearing her white coat or her doctor's scrubs. In running pants and hot-pink sneakers, she doesn't look much like a doctor.

She definitely saw me too. We were staring right at each other until Max yanked my arm. Max backs us out through the crowd so that we've moved a full block in the opposite direction from the runners. Dr. Shabani had paused for a second when she spotted me, but maybe she rejoined the race. I'm hoping there are at least two or three blocks between us now. I crane my neck to see if, by any chance, she might have backtracked to find us.

"Jason, we'd better get away from this race. She probably heard that we snuck out of the hospital. And this race is really crowded. There are a lot of eyeballs here."

"Yeah, but there are also lots of kids," I say. "If we start walking around on our own, we're going to stick out more. At least here, people will think we're with one of these families. We can try to blend in with them. We just have to act normal."

Max bites her lip, flinching.

"Are you saying I'm not normal?" she asks, her voice tight.

"I didn't say that."

"If you're telling me to *act* normal, then that means . . ."

We really need to move, and she's getting picky about my words. I'm not sure what's bothering her.

"Max, you know what I mean. I'm the one who's not normal, so don't be so sensitive. If you're not normal, it's only because you're smarter than everyone else. I wish I had your problems."

Max's eyes turn pink. Her mouth is closed tightly like she's worried something's going to slip out. I don't know what I said that's upset her so much. Max looks tired, more tired than she did when she was hangry. It's after eleven o'clock. We've only been away from the hospital for a few hours, but it's been the kind of few hours that feel like a month.

"Max?"

Max takes a deep breath. She lifts her hat an inch off her head and runs her fingers through her hair. She turns her palm up and flakes of glue fall between her fingers, disappearing onto the sidewalk.

"You don't know what you're talking about," she says quietly.

There it is again. How can I get Max to trust me with whatever it is she's hiding?

"What do you mean?" I ask.

Max is tucking stray hairs behind her ears. She blinks rapidly and clears her throat.

"Let's get moving," she says brightly, but I can hear that her voice is a pretending voice.

"Hey, if there's something that—"

"Max? M.D.? I thought that was you two!"

Max and I both freeze.

Dr. Shabani's out-of-breath voice is unmistakable. We slowly turn around to face her. Max's face is blank. There are no brilliant ideas exploding behind those brown eyes. She's not talking us out of this mess.

"Oh, hey, Dr. Shabani," I say as casually as I can. "What . . . what are you doing here?"

"What am I doing here? What are you two doing here? There wasn't any plan to send you home today, Max. And, you, were they able to locate your parents? Who brought you here?"

These are all very good questions. I wish I had some good answers.

"My mom brought us here to watch the race," Max says. Her nervousness is barely hidden. "I got discharged this morning."

Dr. Shabani has both hands on her hips. Beads of sweat glisten on her furrowed brow. "Discharged? That wasn't even being discussed yesterday." She turns to face me. She's moved in closer, the only runner outside of the barricades. She's getting a few looks for that. "And you? How are you feeling?"

"Awesome," I reply cheerfully. "My head's barely hurting!"

She wipes at her forehead with the back of her hand and shakes her head.

"I've got to be honest with you both. I don't know how it is that the two of you fast friends are out here instead of in the hospital. I'm going to make a quick call." She touches the pouch strapped around her bicep. "Shoot! My friend's got my phone."

Max's eyes are wide as she looks at me and then points her eyeballs off to the right. I press my lips together in silent communication. *No*, I'm telling her in my head.

We're not going to outrun a marathon runner!

"I've got to borrow a phone." She turns to the people around us, trying to figure out who to ask.

"Last chance," Max whispers to me.

The city is not as big and busy as I hoped.

"Excuse me," our doctor calls out. "Does anyone have a phone I could use?"

The people around her pretend not to hear or shake their heads and smile politely. She shoots us a serious look, a warning not to move. She asks again, her hands cupped around her mouth to amplify her voice.

"Excuse me. This is actually pretty urgent. I'm a—"

"Doctor!" There's a shout. It sounds like it's coming from the sea of runners. "Doctor! We need a doctor!"

Dr. Shabani looks back over her shoulder.

"We've got a runner down! Is there a doctor or a paramedic anywhere around here? This man needs help!"

"Oh man, that leg is definitely broken!"

"You two—come with me." Dr. Shabani pushes her way through the gathering crowd. We follow her with dragging feet.

"Poor guy! Tripped over a water bottle!"

People are craning their necks for a closer look at the injured runner. Max and I make eye contact. We are not thinking. We are only doing, moving as quickly as we can. We take three big steps backward and the crowd fills in the space between us and Dr. Shabani. Max and I are shoulder to shoulder, making our way behind the barricades. I think of how we can best disappear.

"Let's stay behind the barricades and try to blend in. We'll move in the same direction as the runners and head uptown to catch the subway train. Dr. Shabani's probably still back there."

We weave through, keeping our heads low and moving slowly enough that it just looks like we're trying to find a better viewing position. There's no sign of the doctor, but we keep looking over our shoulders as if she might just pop up.

We've moved about two blocks uptown when we hear a chorus of beeps and buzzes. A handful of people reach into their pockets or bags and tap on the screen of a cell phone.

"Did you get a text message?" the woman in front of us says to the man next to her. He swipes his thumb across the phone, and I can spot a blue text message box on the screen.

"Amber Alert," I hear the man grumble. He slips his phone back into his jacket pocket.

"How awful," she replies as she shakes her head.

A handful of other people have looked at their phones. They purse their lips or shake their heads or say something to the person next to them.

"Max, what's an Amber Alert?"

Max gives me a look that tells me she doesn't know. I see a father put his arm around the little girl next to him and pull her closer. She looks up at him and smiles. There's a rock in my stomach.

"Maybe it's got something to do with the runner that got injured," Max offers.

It's a good theory. I nudge Max and we keep dodging elbows and backpacks, moving from one crosswalk to the next. I hear bits and pieces of conversations. Together, they shape a story.

"You got the message too?"

"Amber Alert? Yup. I hate seeing these."

"Yeah, it's two. How awful is that!"

"Where from?"

"Not sure. Just says it's a boy and a girl."

Max gasps softly. Our ears prickle at that last comment. Our eyes meet but we don't dare speak.

The Amber Alert has nothing to do with the marathon runners. The Amber Alert, it's dawning on me, is a missing child notice.

"Those poor parents."

"Makes you want to hug your kid a little tighter, doesn't it?"

"And put tracking devices on them. Gosh, I don't know what I'd do."

I cringe, ready for the second when these people will turn around and see my face flaming red. Max is staring into the cracks of the concrete sidewalk.

Did Dr. Shabani report us already? Did the alert give a description or include our pictures? Are our faces going to be on the news?

Max's head is hanging so low it looks like she wants to disappear into the ground.

"Max, maybe we should . . ."

She nods in the direction we were headed, a signal we should keep going. I walk beside her in silence.

Max really looks beat now, and I'm sure she's going to be in huge trouble with her parents. I don't want Max to go any farther. I don't like that this is my fault, but I also don't want to be one more person telling her what she can't do.

With another block behind us, the cell phones have once again disappeared into pockets and handbags. No one's reading about the missing kids, though they're probably thinking about us.

Max ducks into an alley. She leads us behind a dumpster. The smell of rotten food fills my nostrils and turns my stomach. I see a rat's tail disappear behind a stack of cardboard boxes. Max pokes her head out to see if anyone from the street has followed us here.

"Max?"

It's a bright and brilliant day, and here we are, two kids who barely know each other and have nothing in common, hiding in an alley.

"Max. I didn't think it would be like this."

She gives me a weak smile.

"Do you think there's a reward out for finding us?"

"That would be cool," I say, cocking my head to the side. "Maybe I should turn you in."

Max bends down to retie her laces. She says something but I can't make it out since she's talking to the pavement.

"What did you say?"

She stands up and smooths out her purple sweatshirt with two hands as she repeats herself, just loud enough for me to hear this time.

"I'm supposed to have surgery tomorrow."

It is not what I expected to hear.

"I have . . . I have epilepsy, and I'm supposed to have surgery tomorrow."

"Surgery?"

Max nods. She's not pretending anymore.

"I'm not a genius. I'm an epileptic. That's all I am."

"I don't know what that means," I quietly admit.

"It means I have seizures. I get them a lot. My brain gets way too excited and then it goes out of control and it takes over my body. Sometimes my mouth twitches or my hands do weird things. Sometimes it's my whole body.

137

I have to take a bunch of pills that make me feel like I'm moving in slow motion. My parents don't let me do anything because they're always afraid that I'll have another seizure, and they're right. Of course I will. That's what epileptics *do*. And people think that's all we do."

"I've never met anyone with seizures, but you can do lots of stuff."

Max's eyes are pink with a sadness I don't understand.

"Do you know what I hate?" Max asks.

I look at her.

"I really hate that people think I'm dumb or that I'm going to bite my tongue off in front of them."

"People can be pretty dumb," I say, thinking of the people who have asked my mother why she doesn't dress like an Afghan. She says she wears the same clothes people in Afghanistan wear, but people always look shocked.

"Actually, lots of famous people have had seizures."

"Like who?" I ask, curious.

"Like one of the popes, Julius Caesar, Tiki Barber, Lil Wayne . . ."

"Lil Wayne and Tiki Barber have had seizures?"

Max nods. I would have thought Tiki Barber wouldn't have ever had anything more than a sprained ankle.

"Max, how do you make the seizures stop?"

"Medicines. Or they stop on their own. But not everyone knows that. My grandfather thought he was supposed to put a spoon or a stick in my mouth so I wouldn't bite my tongue off. My mom had to tell him that was even more dangerous."

"I wouldn't know what to do if I saw someone having a seizure," I admit.

"There's not much to do. Clear a space around the person and roll her onto her side. Call for help. Don't put anything in her mouth. That's it."

"So, what's the surgery for?"

Max exhales loudly and buries her face in her hands.

"They want to take out the part of my brain that's not working right—the part that's causing seizures."

Surgery on her brain? I feel my own head ache at the thought of that. No wonder Max is so nervous. I wish there were someone else here, someone who would know what to say. How can I tell her not to be scared when I'd be terrified? And if I tell her I'd be scared too, won't that make things worse? I don't have what she needs right now, but I have to say something.

"But that'll help you, right? That will fix the . . . problem, I guess." I am really out of my league in this conversation.

Max wipes a tear away from her cheek with the back of her hand.

"I'm afraid."

"What are you afraid of?"

"What if . . . what if they don't just take out the part

that causes seizures? What if I wake up and I'm not that smart? Or what if I forget all the things that are important to me? What if I never have another seizure again, and what if I don't like that? What if I wake up and they've taken out the part of me that makes me *me*?"

"Is that possible? If that part of your brain isn't working, then that can't be the part that makes you . . . you."

Max is not convinced.

"They think the seizures are all bad," Max says, and I'm guessing she's talking about her parents. "But sometimes the seizures give me things."

"Like what?"

"Sometimes I remember things that happened a really long time ago. Like the pictures on the wall of my grandmother's kitchen before her house burned down. Or the blanket my mother used to wrap around me when we did campfire stories in our backyard. I don't remember everything from when I was four years old, but I remember that stuff. And more."

"That's the treasure box you were telling me about," I say as I start to understand. "So would you rather keep the seizures?"

Max scratches at the back of her head.

"I'd rather keep the good parts. Sometimes I don't take all my medicine because I want to have those memories. My parents think all my memories are bad ones because I was in the hospital so much, but I don't want to forget all of those either."

"Do your parents know you don't take all your medicine?"

"Nope," Max says, and there's a hint of triumph in her voice. "I've been stuffing the extra pills under my mom's geraniums. And I'm happy to report those geraniums haven't had a single seizure since I started doing that."

I laugh. It feels like forever since I last laughed, and I wonder if I'll ever be able to really laugh again. Max smiles. But after a moment, the air between us gets serious again.

"I would be scared too," I tell her.

"You would?"

"Out of my mind scared."

Max lets out a long breath through pursed lips and puffed cheeks. I can see her face relax a little. I guess it's okay that I just told her the truth. The dark shadows beneath her eyes tell me that she probably didn't sleep much last night with the rattling carts and beeping machines on our hospital floor.

"I'd be scared if I were you too," Max says. "I really hope your mom gets to come back."

It's my turn to stare at the ground. I've been trying really hard not to think about how afraid I am that I won't see my mom again or that I won't find Auntie Seema.

That's when a rat pokes his pointy head out from behind the boxes then ducks back in. We both jump and take a quick step backward, laughing at our reactions. A passing dog lets out a small yelp and tugs his leash in our direction. His owner doesn't notice and walks by the alley without seeing us. Two pigeons are perched on the fire escape over our heads, cooing softly. They remind me of home. I can feel my nerves settle a little. There's a rise in the cheering; a new wave of runners must be moving through the hall of people.

"Jason D."

"Yeah, Max?"

Max tilts her head to the sky, a narrow beam of sunlight slipping through the buildings and falling on her face. She closes her eyes and her cheeks turn pink under the glow.

"It's a lot easier to be scared together."

Seventeen

The pigeons have taken off and the rat has disappeared once more. Max comes out from behind the dumpster and peeks out from the alley. We're staring at the backs of people—a sea of jackets, sweaters, and scarves. Max turns to look back at me.

"We don't have much more to go," she says. "The entrance to the zoo is on Sixty-Fourth Street. That's just another block and a half."

"You sound like you're from here."

Max kicks her toe at the pavement playfully.

"I wasn't joking. New York is the coolest."

Now that I've seen New York, I know it's not the violent

and dangerous place my mom thinks it is. I hope I'll get to tell her so.

"I wish my mom didn't think this place was so dangerous."

"More dangerous than Afghanistan?"

"I don't know. All I know is that she really liked our town. She would tell me that all the time. She liked our neighbors and that she could walk to just about everywhere she needed to go. Plus, there's a university near us, and she thinks I'm going to go there and become a doctor or an engineer or something."

"She's picked out where you're going to college already?" Max asks incredulously.

"Yeah," I say with a small smile. Now that I know about Max's seizures, I feel like I know her better. It really was as if I didn't know her full story without knowing about her seizures.

I remember her words. *I'm not a genius. I'm an epileptic. That's all I am.*

That doesn't seem right to me. She may be an epileptic, but that's not all she is.

"What's your mom like?" Max asks.

"My mom is . . . well, she's my mom." How can I tell the story of who my mom is with just a few words? "She's cool even if she is pretty strict. She likes singing along with the radio but gets all the words wrong. She wants me

144

to be American, like, really American, so she bought me books of nursery rhymes and lullabies when I was little so she could teach them all to me. It was stuff she'd never learned when she was a kid so it was strange for her, especially the 'Rock-a-bye Baby' song."

"What's strange about that song?"

"What's strange about a bedtime song where a baby falls out of a tree with his whole cradle? Why would you sing that to a baby about to go to sleep?"

"Oh," Max says, and her lips stay in that perfect O shape for a moment before she speaks again. "I guess it is a little creepy."

With every city block we cross, I learn something about Max and she learns something about me.

"What do you think is going to happen to your mom?"

I can't answer that question. I've tried to keep moving so I won't have to think about it. But of course, it's there, the thought that she's on her way to a place that's always in the news and never for a good reason. I wonder if the same bad people who took away my dad are going to find out she's back.

But my mom's tough. When we lost our furniture in an apartment fire, she slept on the floor and made me a bed out of all our blankets. She stays up late at night to read my schoolbooks so she can help me with my homework. She's the one who taught me how to fix a leaking faucet, and before I started doing it, she was the one would get up early on snow days to clear the steps of our building and a path to the street. She always seems to wake up when I do, even in the middle of the night.

"My mom's kind of a warrior," I say with a wry smile, because I've just realized that's exactly what she is. And realizing how tough she is makes me hopeful that she's going to find a way to get back to me like she promised.

"A warrior!" Max exclaims. I can see a pause in her step, and I know she's considering the word, trying it on. She says it once more, learning something about herself, as we cross another block. "I like that. A warrior."

We trod on, Max pausing every ten minutes or so to take a break (though she pretends to be checking her watch or retying her sneakers). We keep our heads low and fall into a steady pace, our tired feet hitting the pavement in synchrony.

When I ask Max what time it is, she doesn't answer. She's standing in front of a store window.

"Max, we've got to cross the street again. You okay?"

When Max still doesn't answer, I get nervous. What am I going to do if she has a seizure?

"Sorry, just spaced out for a minute." Maybe she can see the panic on my face, because she tries to reassure me. "Seriously, Jason D. I'm fine."

The white stick figure on the crosswalk sign tells us to cross. When we're back on the sidewalk, Max points to a cluster of trees on the other side of the avenue.

"See that?" she asks, turning to look at me.

"Central Park," I whisper. It feels like we've just spotted the ocean.

I always thought New York City was all tall buildings and crowded streets. What I'm looking at is nothing like that. Standing at the park's edge, I can see it's a world within a world. A wall of trees frames its borders. I can't see through them, even after we've crossed the street. In front of the trees, as if guarding this entrance to the park, is an enormous golden statue atop a tall concrete base. I squint against the sun's glare. It's a figure of a man, straight-backed and grim-faced, riding a horse. The man's cape billows behind in an invisible wind. A stone-faced woman stands before him and his horse, her right arm raised toward the sky and a feather as long as her torso in her left hand. She's got a garland on her head and graceful angel wings.

"That looks so real," I whisper. I can almost see the horse's nostrils flare.

Max is less impressed but lingers while I take in the statue. Though it's made of metal, the horse's legs look muscular and rippled. The female figure wears a draping gown. She looks like an angel or a goddess out of some kind of mythology story.

"We can't hang out here, Jason D."

The unmoving horse has a curled front leg, as if he's about to trot off. His neck is so thick I could barely have circled it with my two arms. What would it feel like to ride such a powerful animal? I picture myself charging ahead on its back with my head held high and the guardian angel pointing me onward.

"Victory," Max says, seeing how captivated I am.

I turn to face her.

"What?"

"She's Victory. That's what the plaque says." She looks back over her shoulder, and I follow her gaze. Five people are crossing the street. They're talking to one another when one of them looks over in our direction, an expression of curiosity crossing her face.

Have they seen the alert about the missing kids? Max is right. We've got to keep moving.

We cross the square quickly and duck into the green sanctuary. The sounds of people and cars fade. Dry grass crunches under the soles of our sneakers, and a light breeze rustles the leaves of the soaring trees.

"Hey, Max." The statue reminded me of a riddle. "A cowboy rode into town on Friday. Two days later he rides out on Friday."

"A riddle—now?"

I nod.

"Fine then. Two days later ... still Friday." She makes me repeat the riddle and refuses to let me tell her the answer. When I think she'll give up, she stops in her tracks and points at me.

"The horse's name is Friday!"

In a patch of bushes to my left, there's a snap, and my heart skips a beat guessing at what might have just scampered away. A bushy gray tail passes on my left, but it's gone before I can tell. Max, knees high, continues to make her way across a low hill studded with trees. We're walking toward a glimmering pond on the other side.

I am disappearing into a fairy tale forest. Whether the forest is enchanted or haunted, I don't know yet.

Eighteen

ax walks over to the edge of the pond and takes a seat on a bed of stones. She puts the backpack beside her and sits cross-legged. There are no people in sight, so I do the same. The water glows green gold with the reflection of the surrounding trees. It looks like the trio of mallards is gliding through painted water.

"Think you'll ever get to go back home?" Max asks. She's facing the water, as if she might be asking her question of the ducks.

"I don't know," I say. "Maybe one day, if my mom comes back."

"Behind my house, there's a wooded area with an old well and a lake. It's like a private forest. I drop pennies into the well and make wishes. And there's this one cluster of trees that comes together in a circle just big enough for me to sit and stretch out my legs. I know it sounds crazy, but I could sit in that tree circle for hours. It doesn't have walls or anything fancy in it, but it feels like the safest place in the world."

That kind of reminds me of how I feel when I climb up to the roof of our building. The well she's mentioned reminds me of another riddle.

"What is it that goes with a wide-mouthed grin and returns with falling tears?"

Max looks over at me, a faint smile on her face. After a moment, she shrugs her shoulders and waits for me to tell her.

"A bucket in the well."

"Ah, that's a good one," she says. I can tell she's imagining an empty bucket drifting down into the dark well and coming back, water sloshing out of its sides like tears.

"What do you do when you sit in the circle of trees?"

"Promise not to laugh?"

"C'mon, Max."

Max grins and continues. She knows by now I wouldn't laugh at anything she does.

"Sometimes I pretend it's actually in Central Park and I'm right there in the middle of New York City. Sometimes I just go there to read. On the Fourth of July, there are fireworks at the lake. My parents don't usually let me watch because they're afraid the flashing lights will start a seizure, but last year they let me try. I took a blanket out there and watched the colors light the sky."

I can picture Max with her head resting on her overlapping hands, staring upward at the night sky and seeing fireworks for the first time. My mother and I always watch the fireworks from the rooftop of our building with Ms. Raz and our other neighbors. It wouldn't be much fun if I couldn't join them.

"Now that you're in Central Park, does it feel like your tree circle back home?"

"Nothing feels like home."

I know what she means. Max looks down at her hands. I've been curious but didn't want to ask until now.

"What happened to your hands, Max?"

Max turns her hands over then squeezes them together.

"I was afraid I wouldn't remember the way to my tree circle again. So the day before we were going to the hospital, I took my dad's carving knife and marked little arrows into the trees so I could find my way back to it. Then I felt bad that I was hurting the trees. None of this was their fault. My parents had to pull me off a tree. I wouldn't let go of it."

She closes her hands into fists.

"My mom couldn't get all the splinters out. The doctors in the hospital had to do it."

"Do you really think you'd forget the way to your favorite place?"

Max shrugs. "I didn't want to take the chance," she says simply.

I had let go of my mother too easily. Why hadn't I put up as much of a fight as Max?

"What about you? Where's your favorite place to be?"

I'd never thought about my favorite place to be. I like sitting on the rooftop with my pigeons. I like going home after school. And sometimes I like hanging out in the laundromat with my mother. Then there's the park that we go to, with a paper bag filled with my mom's spiced potatoes in folded bread and bottles of juice. All my favorite places are right around my home, and I can't go back to any of them.

"I'm still working on figuring that out, I guess."

A squirrel bounces playfully from branch to branch in a nearby tree. He pauses and meets my eye for a brief second. The squirrel flies about four feet down to the earth. I hear a crunch and a snap, and he vanishes into the soft bed of fallen leaves.

"I don't think I could have told any of my friends back home about this stuff," I tell Max sheepishly. She knows by "stuff" I mean what's happened to my mother. "Even when I found out about my mom's papers, I didn't want to tell anyone. Just seemed like that could change everything."

Max nods.

"My second-grade teacher used to tell the kids to be extra nice to me because I was a *brave* and *special* girl— as if I couldn't tell what kind of *special* she meant. I was as popular as extra homework that year. But I fixed that problem."

"How'd you fix it?"

Max laughs at her memory.

"I brought in a jar of live spiders. And a jar of worms. I had holes punched in the lids to let in air. Then, before class started, I super-glued the jars to my desk. My teacher totally flipped. She tried to be cool while she asked me why I'd brought in spiders and worms but her voice was as squeaky as a mouse. I told her it's what *special* and *brave* kids do."

"Did you seriously do that?"

Max nods and holds up her hand as if she's taking an oath.

"If you ever meet Ms. Kaplan, you can ask her yourself."

"I never thought being brave was a bad thing," I say. "But I guess if you're being brave it's only because something bad is happening."

154

Max doesn't say anything after that. She pulls her notebook out of her backpack and fishes around for her pen.

I look at the water and the ducks. I watch how the leaves bend and curl with the breeze and the way the trunks of trees cast long, dramatic shadows. The sun is high in the sky, which tells me the hours are passing quickly. We've got to get moving.

As if Max has sensed what I'm thinking, she zips up her backpack. The notebook is gone. She presses her hands against the rocks and pushes herself to stand. I tilt my head back and look up at her. Standing against the bright sun, I see only her silhouette. She looks tall and brave and strong. I want to tell her but I know now that's not what she wants to hear.

Instead, I stand up too and we start walking again. We stay close to the trees, believing their trunks can hide us from the world. Max has promised that the zoo is close.

"Max, you're right!"

We're staring at an entry made of three brick arches. At the center is a tower with the round face of a clock. It's already noon. With every minute that ticks by, Max and I are in bigger and bigger trouble.

Parents are pushing babies in strollers. Teenagers walk in groups. A small chunk of New York City's millions is here today. It's an odd thing to see a crowd now. I'm not sure if we can disappear into them or if we're going to be spotted by them.

Max's eyes are wide and bright, too close to her simple wish to believe anything could go wrong now. With all that's happened since Friday, I can still feel happy for her that she's made it this far. At least she'll be able to visit the zoo before her surgery.

"Uh-oh," I moan. Max stops short. We've both just spotted the sign for ticket booths.

"Do you think the tickets are free?" Max asks.

"Tickets usually aren't," I say slowly. I hate to think we won't make it past this point, but we only have sixteen dollars left in Max's bag. I used up everything I had on my train ticket into the city.

Max is stretching herself, standing on tiptoes and craning her neck to see over the fences and trees and into the zoo's enclosures. She bites her lip and looks around. We can't just hang out here, wondering. There are no ticket machines as far as I can see, so I head straight for the booths.

"Jason D," Max calls out after me. "Where are you going?"

"Hello," I say cheerily to the gray-haired man behind the booth. "Are kids' tickets free? My friend and I were wondering."

"Your friend," he repeats, searching behind me.

"My friend," I say, pointing my thumb in Max's direction.

"How old are you two?" the man asks. My palms get sweaty. Why is he asking? Then my eyes fall upon a sign next to the ticket window. Ticket prices are based on age. Children's tickets cost thirteen dollars. That's cheaper than adult tickets but far from free.

"We're both children," I say in my most adult voice.

"Only kids under two get in free," he says. He's got the same concerned look on his face as the man walking the two dogs and Dr. Shabani at the race. Maybe I'm acting too nervous.

"Well, that makes sense. I've never seen a two-year-old carry around much cash," I say with a casual smile.

"I suppose not," he replies, mildly amused. "Any adults here with you?"

I've gotten myself into this mess. I've got to get myself out.

"Sure, my . . . my parents are here with me."

Why did I say that?

"Great. Why don't you have them come up and buy the tickets?"

I nod, giving the man something close to a smile before I turn and walk away. My eyes burn.

My parents are here with me.

Those words have never before come out of my mouth. They've left a strange aftertaste—partly sweet and partly bitter.

"Did you get the tickets?" Max asks excitedly. I clear my throat and squint, trying to send the tears back.

"No," I say. My voice sounds thick and strange. "We need an adult with us."

"What's wrong?" Max puts a hand on my forearm.

"Nothing." I move away, not wanting to be touched.

"Hey, Jason D, you can talk to me. Remember?"

I do remember, but I can't do this now. I'm afraid of what will happen if I let myself think about it too much. It was bad enough living with just a photo of my dad. Now I don't have either of my parents. Max and I are tucked against the side of a looming archway, our backs to the traffic of people.

"Jason D, you can't give up now," Max says gently. "You're going to get to your aunt's house, and I bet your mom's already called to find out if you're with her."

I let out a deep breath and nod, trying to ignore the heavy feeling in my chest. Maybe a detour through the zoo is exactly what I need.

"We need tickets. And they're not free. They're thirteen dollars each, and we've only got sixteen."

"I think I might have an idea." Max has her eye on a

158

group of green-shirted adults and kids huddling by the entrance. There are about fifty kids, middle-schoolers by my guess, and four adults. One woman is on a cell phone. A man and a woman are talking to each other. Another woman points into the air with one finger, counting the many heads before her.

Max opens her backpack and takes the bills out of her owl wallet.

"Follow me," she says, walking quickly. The zoo is close to the edge of the park, so within moments we're back out on a wide avenue. Max marches right up to a kiosk with T-shirts and souvenirs. The dark-haired man inside gives a nod.

"How much for that green Statue of Liberty shirt, please?" Max asks with confidence.

"Fifteen dollars," the man says. I can see he's more than comfortable doing business with us, unlike the man at the ticket booth.

"Max, that'll leave us with one dollar!" I point out, but Max ignores me.

"I'll take it. And I don't need a bag."

As soon as she turns her back to the kiosk, she turns the shirt inside out. Lady Liberty disappears and Max slips the shirt over the one she's already wearing. Now we're both wearing green.

"Hurry up," she says, and starts jogging back to the

zoo's entrance. When we return, I see the crowd of green shirts getting ready to head through a side gate. I guess they're allowed to skip the turnstiles because there are so many of them.

"Stick close," Max says, and I follow her. We linger in the background and then press ourselves into the herd of green shirts, not in the back where we'd be noticed, but coming in from the side so we're quickly surrounded by them. The chaperones call out instructions, and the kids are chatting. They're all speaking a language we don't understand.

We make it through, and tall black gates close behind us. The group spreads out, and Max and I let ourselves drift to the edge. When the adults huddle around an unfolded map of the zoo, we leave them behind.

"Not bad, eh?" Max asks with a grin. She takes the green shirt off, rolls it up, and stuffs it into her backpack.

I find myself smiling, despite the rock in my chest.

We walk down the path to a large, glass-enclosed pool with a rock island at its center. Through the glass, I make out the shapes of three sea lions doing laps around the rocks, their flippers stretched out and noses pointed forward. Small children have their faces pressed against the glass, which is a couple of feet away from the pool. There's a splash, and one of the sea lions breaks through the surface and lands on a flat stone. His body is smooth and shiny like polished glass. When he wiggles his whiskers from side to side, I laugh.

I look at Max and see a thin smile and tired eyes.

"Let's go this way," she says with her eyes on the path to our left.

There are kids around us. I wonder if we look normal to them, as if there's nothing special or brave about us.

"In here," Max whispers. We slip into a tall building and are suddenly in a tropical forest with bamboo trees and wide-leafed plants. The leaves are bigger than my head and unlike anything I've ever seen. We walk along a boardwalk, the kind that might connect two treehouses. Perched on a crooked branch, a brightly colored parrot stretches its wings. A bird with shimmery turquoise feathers swivels its head curiously as we pass by. There are vines I could imagine Tarzan swinging from, crossing this small jungle with one holler.

We follow the boardwalk and see a set of stairs leading deeper into this blooming rain forest. On the vertical faces of the steps, I see words that form a sentence. Slowly, I recognize a line from a story I used to read in the library, the one about a boy who got in trouble and was sent to his room without dinner. The words are painted in white and make me think of the shadow creatures my mom made on the walls of our bedroom at night.

I climb the steps with Max, the story at our feet. This

forest looks just like the one that grew out of bedposts and wallpaper. I feel like I've stepped into a fantasy.

Max stops short in front of me. She puts a finger to her lips and then points up into the canopy above us. It takes me a second to spot it, but then I see what's made her pause. A peacock sits across from a bird as yellow as the sun. From behind a glass pane, I see a brilliant green snake coiled around a tree branch. His scaly back is striped with white marks that read like a warning label. A shiver runs down my spine, and I'm relieved when we step outside again.

"Snakes creep me out," Max admits.

"But not spiders and worms?" I ask.

"Excuse me? Totally different," Max insists, sounding almost offended.

We enter the Temperate Territory. I notice Max has to double her steps once in a while to keep up with me, so I slow down. When I do, I notice a creature I've never seen before. Perched on a tree limb is an animal with the face of a fox and the paws of a bear. He is sleeping, his head resting on the branch, and his bushy, ringed tail dangling beneath him.

"What is that?"

"Oh, I've read about this guy. Friend, that is the legendary red panda," Max declares with her hands on her hips. I can picture her as a great wildlife biologist—the kind who will make smart television shows for kids. "Not to be confused with Kung Fu Panda or the panda you had pictured in your mind. They only eat the most tender bamboo shoots, along with some insects and fruits."

The zoo is filled with tall trees, their leaves the colors of a sunset. Beyond the treetops, there's a banner of skyscrapers looming overhead. Both are pretty impressive.

Next, we're at the snow monkeys. Two monkeys sit on a rock formation overlooking a pool of water. They are hugging their knees the way small children do.

"Look at these guys. Do you know they have emotions and relationships just like—"

Max pauses. Where I thought there were only two monkeys, I now see three. The third is small, and clings to its mother's chest. It turns to look over its shoulder, and its red leathery face stands out against the tan of their fur. The father tilts his head in, bringing himself a breath closer to his family. The mother yawns, baring her yellow teeth before she nuzzles her head against the baby on her chest.

Max and I have pretended a lot of things today. We've pretended to be raising money. We've pretended to have parents right behind us. We've pretended to be strong and brave and normal.

But we cannot, no matter how hard we try, pretend that something inside each of us doesn't crash with anger and hurt when we see these three snow monkeys looking perfectly content just sitting together as a family.

Nineteen

Max decides she's seen enough at the zoo. It's time to get back to our original mission. We head toward an exit, and with all the parents and kids wandering through the zoo paths, no one notices two long-faced kids leave.

"This way is uptown," Max says. "It's only nine blocks from here to Seventy-Fourth Street, and then we just have to find the right building."

We stay just inside the park, walking close to bushes and trees. Max is moving more slowly now. She must be pretty hungry. I know I am. But the dollar we have left isn't going to get us very much.

Max reaches into the front pocket of her backpack and

pulls out her cell phone. She presses a side button and I see the screen light up as it turns on.

"What are you doing?"

"I just want to see if I have any messages."

There are seventeen.

Max starts to listen to them as we walk. She's got her eyes on the ground, but I can see her face in profile. She bites her lip and presses a button to listen to the next message. I can hear her mother's voice and even make out a few frantic words. *I'm going out of my mind. Please please please call me, Maxi. I need to know you're okay. Call me or call your dad, but please just call us.*

In the last message, there is nothing but "we love you." It is said between sobs, and I feel sorry for Max's mother, who obviously is really worried about her.

"You should call her," I say gently. I stare at the ground too, because I'm basically telling Max that her adventure is at its end. It's not an easy thing to say, but we've come a long way together, and I feel like I should be able to say this much.

"I know," she whispers. She puts the phone in her pocket. She's trying hard not to cry, but it's not easy. Listening to the sound of her mom's voice has me on the verge of tears too. Max rubs her face with both hands and turns away from me.

"Just tell her you're okay and that we're close by their hotel."

"I'll call her in a couple of minutes," she says determinedly, "when we find your aunt's building. You won't need me after that."

As much as I want to be with Auntie Seema, a part of me doesn't want to say good-bye to Max. I wonder if I'll ever see her after today. We pause before we slip out of the park and onto the sidewalk. The trees and hills have become our friends, helping us stay hidden from the millions of city eyes.

With the park behind us, we start walking down Seventy-Fourth Street. I am looking at all the buildings, trying to spot the one that looks like the building in the picture. I see fire escapes and big windows that look wrong.

We walk three blocks. Then we walk four. When we hit the fifth block, I'm really worried we might not be in the right place. This was the address I ripped off the box, so where's the building?

"Jason D, it's not any of these?"

"I don't think so."

Max rubs the middle of her forehead while I look around once more.

"No. No, it's definitely not any of these."

"Let's try the next block."

This is the right street. There's a green sign on the corner with *74th* written on it. I fight the urge to yell out Auntie Seema's name and see if any of the window curtains pull back to answer.

"I don't know, Max. It's not what it's supposed to be." My voice is trembling.

Max is at my side.

"You need to stay cool, Jason D." She kicks her feet up as we walk and issues a quiet warning in a sing-song voice. "Peo-ple are look-ing."

"This can't be happening."

"Do you want to stop?" Max suggests, but I shake my head. Auntie Seema has to be somewhere around here. Fifteen minutes later, we're looking at a busy road. There are crowds of people, many with poster boards in their hands. There is shouting and cheering and even what sounds like a bullhorn in the distance.

"No way," Max moans.

"They're here," I say in disbelief. They are still running. The stream of runners is much lighter than what we'd seen this morning, but these runners are still at it, feet pounding the asphalt and foreheads glistening with sweat.

Beyond the runners, I see there is water. That tells me something else. We've gone as far as we can on this street and I did not see Auntie Seema's building.

"Max?"

"Yeah?"

"Can we just sit for a minute?"

"Yeah." Max was looking exhausted at the zoo, but right now I need this break more than she does.

We sit under a bus shelter.

"It's over. I'm sorry I wasted your time, Max." I wish I had stuffed that cardboard address into my pocket instead of my backpack. What if I've remembered it wrong?

"You didn't waste my time, Jason D."

I swallow hard.

Max takes out her notebook and pen. I don't feel like talking, so I let her write and keep my back turned to her so that she can't see my face. Everything's gone so wrong, and I don't know what my next move will be or even if I have a next move.

I stare at the concrete.

Cars drive by, horns honking almost randomly. Bicycles whiz past us. I see a man pushing a shopping cart full of old plastic bags. He's wearing a beat-up jacket that looks like it was made out of an old comforter.

I stare past the runners and see a tugboat in the water. It floats by slowly and reminds me of a riddle Mr. Fazio told me about a boat. How did that one go? I think it was that two sailors were standing on opposite ends of a ship.

Then I remember the rest.

Two sailors were standing on opposite ends of a ship. One was looking west and the other was looking east. They could see each other clearly. How is that possible?

That one took me a few minutes. Mr. Fazio thought he had me stumped that day. He was ready to open up his newspaper and go back to reading when I pulled an edge down to look him in the eye as I told him the answer.

The two sailors were looking at each other.

I'm thinking of this riddle now and a slow realization hits me.

"Max."

"Yup."

"We're on the east side of Central Park."

"Uh, yeah, I guess so."

"So what's on the other side of the park?"

"Not sure. A museum, I think. And more buildings."

I'm on my feet.

"It's the west side, Max. I bet Seventy-Fourth Street continues on the other side of the park. That must be where Auntie Seema's apartment is!"

Max is up too. Maybe she's disappointed that she, as a New York City expert, didn't realize this.

"You're brilliant, Jason D," she says brightly.

I want to believe her, but there's a little voice inside me that wonders if I'm right.

Shoulders bumping against each other, we walk with determination.

If I'm right, all we have to do is walk a straight line across the park to come out on Seventy-Fourth Street on the other side. We've wasted some time on this side of the island, but we're making up for it now.

Yellow taxis pass by and we groan, wishing we could hop into one and search out the house from the comfort of a back seat. I keep my eyes on the buildings on this block to be sure I haven't missed Auntie Seema's home. Nothing comes close to the photograph.

"We're almost at the park again. I remember seeing that green door pretty soon after we left the zoo."

I've never had a friend like Max before, a friend who tries to make me feel better even when she could use a little cheering on too.

"Just tell me if you want to take a break or if—"

Max takes the lead, as if to prove to me just how fine she is.

I look at Max. I see a girl my height. Her shoulders are pulled back and she's got her thumbs hooked under the straps of her backpack. Her ponytail is pulled through the hole in the back of her cap and bounces with each step. I can't see her face, but I can guess at the expression she's making right now. Lips pressed to a line and eyes straight ahead. I like that about Max—she only smiles when there's something to smile about.

Will her surgery really change her the way she thinks it will?

I don't want Max to change. I don't think her parents would want her to change either. I remember the panic in her mother's voice. I can't make her go any farther, even if I don't want to go the rest alone.

"Max, we're going to be close to your parents' hotel soon," I begin. "I can get across the park on my own."

Max doesn't answer.

I see my friend against a backdrop of green. We're two avenues away from the park and nearing the next cross-walk. The straps of Max's backpack start to slide as her shoulders slope downward.

"Let me carry the bag, Max," I offer, and put my hands on the backpack to help slip it off her. Just as I do, I see her head tilt slightly to the left and her knees buckle.

"Max!"

I lean forward and instinctively wrap my arms around Max's trunk. We fall to the ground together, her landing halfway on me as my left side hits the concrete. Thank-fully, my arm cushions her fall, and her head doesn't hit the pavement.

I scramble back up and kneel at her side.

"Max, are you okay?" I shout.

I can see she's not.

Her arms and legs are twitching. Her half-closed eyelids are fluttering, and the muscles of her face look tight.

"Max, please don't!"

But Max can't stop what's happening any more than I can. I remember what she told me and see that it's true. Her body's not under her control anymore. It's like some angry puppeteer's taken charge. Her lips are pale, and her arms and legs are jerking. The worst part is, instead of being with her parents or in a hospital surrounded by doctors and nurses who can help her, she's having a seizure on a concrete sidewalk.

And it's all my fault.

Twenty

"*H*ey, what happened to your friend?"

I look up and see two people standing over me. My eyes are blurred with tears so I can't make out their faces.

"Max!" I holler again, my hands planted on the concrete. She's still twitching. "Someone please help!"

My call is answered as someone pulls me away by my elbows. Another person is barking out that we need an ambulance. I am standing against a building, the back of my head pressed against the bricks, watching adults take my place over Max.

I don't want to look. I don't want to see my friend thrashing around, that lost look on her face.

And I don't want to see the people standing over Max. I don't want to see them stare or look away or cover their children's eyes, because that's what they're all doing right now.

I want to be anywhere but here.

"Did you call 911?"

I'm waiting to hear someone say she's okay. I'm waiting to hear Max announce it's over and that she's back to her normal self.

"Hold her down—you've got to stop it."

"Is anyone here a doctor?"

"The ambulance is on its way, but the marathon's made a mess of traffic. Oh man, this isn't good! Put a stick between her teeth so she doesn't bite her tongue. Someone grab a stick!"

No, I think.

In a blink, I'm pushing my way through the ring of adult bodies. They're hovering over Max, and someone's got two hands on Max's jerking arms, pinning her to the ground.

"Stop it!" I shout.

"We're trying to stop it, kid. Just back up and let us handle this." The circle of people tightens, and I realize they're trying to squeeze me back out. I won't let that happen. I can't let that happen.

"Stop what you're doing! You're going to hurt her!"

"Is she your sister? Where's your mom?"

I elbow my way closer to Max and pull those hands off her arms. I've never been so loud speaking to adults, but this is Max they're talking about. Max needs them to hear me.

"She's having a seizure. Don't hold her down. Roll her onto her side and don't even think about putting a stick or anything else in her mouth unless you want to choke her."

Something, possibly the anger in my voice, makes them listen to me. My hands are trembling.

Please stop, I pray silently. *Please make it stop.*

When I open my eyes again, Max is groaning softly. Her body has stopped thrashing, and her arms and legs lie motionless. She looks okay. She looks like she's sleeping.

"Is it over?"

"Man, I hope so. Poor thing."

I can hear the relief in their voices. I count five adults— five people who came when I called for help, even if they didn't exactly know what to do.

I stare at Max's face, watching the pink slowly return to her lips, when a long shadow is cast over her. I look up and see a blue uniform. My heart hammers away in my chest. There's no mistaking things this time. This is not a train conductor or a security guard or even a late Hallow-een costume. This is a real live police officer looming over

176

me, his eyes hidden by sunglasses.

"Is she okay?" He leans in and checks her pulse by pressing two fingers to the inside of her wrist. Reassured, he stands again and starts asking the adults questions about what happened.

"Looking better than a second ago. We're waiting on the ambulance. This fella right here knew just what to do, though."

"Good job, kid!"

Someone slaps my shoulder. I shrug and look at the ground. A man pushes his way through and taps the policeman on his shoulder.

"Officer, we're so glad you showed up when you did! We're visiting—it's our first time in New York City, and this is way more excitement than we'd planned on having! Can we bother you with a question? Our son left his teddy bear on the subway, and we were wondering how we could file a report . . ."

The police officer has one eye on Max as he listens to the man reporting a missing stuffed animal. Looking past him, I realize that this officer did not come in a police car. A few feet away there's a magnificent-looking horse with a shiny, sable coat. She whips her tail and lifts one foot briefly, almost like a wave.

I turn my attention back to Max. My heart is thumping

in my chest nervously. I should turn myself in to this officer, but I'm not ready to do that. I'm not ready to give up yet.

Max is blinking rapidly. The fog is lifting, just as it did for me in the hospital's emergency room after my concussion.

"Jason D," she whispers. The look on my face must tell her to look around and figure out what's happened. Her eyes rove upward and find the police officer. I can see her forehead wrinkle with frustration.

"Are you all right?" I say quietly so that only she can hear me.

"Mm-hmm," she replies with the slightest nod.

"There's an ambulance coming. You're going to be fine." I put my hand on hers.

"Jason."

"Yeah, Max?"

"I'm glad you were here."

"I'm glad too."

"The police . . ."

"I don't think he knows who we are."

I look over at the officer. He's recording the names of the people who had stopped to help Max.

Max closes her eyes; her lashes make dark half circles.

"Jason D," she whispers, eyes fluttering softly. "Take my backpack and just walk away. They're not even paying attention."

"No way. I'm not leaving you," I say, shaking my head. "I can't just walk away when you're like this."

"Not my first seizure, Jason D. Not the first time I've been like this." Her words are heavy and slow, like she's speaking underwater.

That's true, but I don't want her to feel alone.

"But these people don't know what to do for you."

"I'll tell them," she says with determination.

I don't doubt that.

Her eyelids are still heavy, but color is slowly returning to her cheeks. She's got faint freckles I never noticed before. I put my hand over hers.

"What kind of friend just leaves when . . . when—"

"The ambulance will be here any second now, and so will my parents," Max insists, her words coming out slow and a little unclear. "Come on. We rocked it today. There's still a chance for victory."

Victory, the winged figure from the statue. The muscled horse behind her.

Red twirling lights approach. An ambulance has pulled up to the curb, and one uniformed paramedic is pulling a stretcher out of the back of the vehicle while another is bent over Max, taking my place. The police officer crouches down too.

When I stand up, Max's backpack is in my hands. I slip my arms through the straps.

The corners of Max's mouth turn up in the slightest hint of a smile. That's when I know she'll be okay if I go, maybe even better if she knows I'm still pressing on. The second line of the riddle echoes in my head.

Two days later, he rides out on Friday.

This can't be me thinking about doing this. I'm not the kind of kid who does things like this.

I can't see Max anymore. She's somewhere behind the two paramedics, the police officer, three of the good Samaritans who stopped to help, and the little boy who left his teddy bear on the subway. On top of that, more people are now joining the circle of onlookers because everyone's a little curious about what's happening.

The horse snorts and looks my way. It feels like the pieces of a puzzle falling into place.

I'm not thinking. I'm not even doing. It's just *happening.*

No one notices me inch my way to Friday, hidden from view by the ambulance with its swirling lights. No one notices how I first touch her silky coat of hair and feel her muscles ripple under my hand. The sculpture was cool, but the real thing is amazing. The horse lowers her head as I approach, and I feel my spine straighten. As Max is lifted off the ground and transferred onto a stretcher, no one sees me plant one foot on a fire hydrant and grab the horse's reins. I hop up and slide my foot into a stirrup.

I swing my leg around to straddle the horse. I have the reins in my hands and lean forward to press my body against her thick, strong neck. Her ears flicker, as if waiting for instruction.

I've come this far, I think. *There's nothing to lose now.*

"Come on, Friday. Let's go!"

Twenty-One

A storm of shouting erupts behind me. I think I can hear the police officer's shouts in the mix, but mostly I just hear my own panicked groans.

"Oh no . . . whoa . . . watch out, girl!"

When Friday raised her hoof at me, she probably assumed I had ridden a horse before. By now she's probably figured out how wrong she was to assume anything. My bottom thumps against the saddle like one of those rubber balls tied to a wooden paddle. The general in that statue and every cowboy I've ever seen on television make it look so easy.

It's not.

I'm halfway down the block when I dare to look over my shoulder.

"Oh man," I mumble. The police officer is running toward me while everyone else watches, hands over their mouths. The horse is jogging or trotting or skipping or whatever it is that horses do. I'm trying to keep my balance when she takes one extra-big hop, lifting me a couple of inches into the air. When I fall back into the saddle, my leg slaps against her flank and she whinnies.

She's clearly read my leg hitting her as a sign to speed up. It's hard to unkick her, and I can't think of how else to tell her this was a quicker getaway than I'd imagined.

"Whoa . . . whoa . . . whoaaaaaaa!" I yell. She has taken off down the street with my unintended encouragement. I think the cars have stopped, but it's hard to tell with my eyes mostly closed. I'm hugging Friday's neck as tightly as I can, but I'm still being thrashed around like a rag doll, prepared to be thrown to the ground any second now. She veers right and then left. I don't know which street I'm on, and can't begin to figure it out.

I twist the reins around my arms until I'm feeling a lot more secure. I look back again, and the police officer is a blue dot against a blur of cars. He's still coming after me, but the distance between us is growing.

Where to now? Should I just ride through the park? A

boy on a horse is pretty noticeable. I could try to disappear underground, but I can't exactly ride Friday onto a subway car. I'm going to have to get off this horse and duck back into the crowd.

Max's bag slaps against my back. I shout at Friday to stop, tugging on the reins. She snorts but I feel her step ease up a bit. I give the reins one desperate pull.

"Please!" I yell. "Please stop!"

Friday eases her gait and my body starts to relax. I lift my head and spot the dark-green railing that marks the subway station just up ahead. This is my best shot. The police officer must have taken a shortcut because he's back in view, but nearly two blocks away. Friday comes to a stop, her hooves tapping against the asphalt even as she stands. On our left side, there's a stack of empty milk crates on the sidewalk. I unwind the leather reins from my forearms and nervously slide one leg up and over Friday's saddle while I inch myself to the crates.

"Just hold still one second," I whisper.

I hop off the crates and take a deep breath. A shopkeeper is staring at me, and so are two trendy-looking men and a woman in athletic gear clutching an infant to her chest. I brush at my pants and give them a small wave like all is right with the world.

I start to walk toward the subway entrance. I don't dare run because I don't want them to think they should stop me. I have to stay calm. They seem too stunned to act, but that won't last long. I make my way down the stairs, taking note that I'm at the Eighty-Sixth Street station. Coming from the bright afternoon, the subway entrance feels dark and cavelike. A few of the overhead lightbulbs have blown out and need to be replaced. There are ticket machines and a subway map displayed against the white-tiled walls. A train pulls into the station, and just past the turnstiles, clusters of people are waiting for the subway doors to open. The glass booth in the center of the station is empty, and there's no one around watching me. I'm still close enough that I can hear shouting coming from aboveground.

I look at the turnstile and see how easy it would be to duck under the metal bars and slip onto that train just as it leaves the station. The officer is still out of view and won't know where I've gone.

It's a pretty decent plan, I think, even as I consider my options. I take a look around the train station, feeling like I'm up against a ticking clock, when a riddle interrupts my thoughts.

I can only live where there is light, but I die if the light shines on me. What am I?

A heartbeat later, the police officer flies down the stairs, his feet barely landing on the steps. He leaps over the turnstile like an Olympian and pushes his way through the people bursting off the train. Some of them look annoyed when his shoulders bump against theirs, but they swallow their anger when they realize he's a police officer. The cop scans left and right and hears the mechanical voice warning passengers to stand clear of the closing doors. He steps onto the train and moves quickly through the subway car, looking for me.

The subway train starts to move out of the station, slipping into a large black hole. The officer looks confused, like someone's just pulled a rabbit out of a paper bag. The people on the train look puzzled too. They're not sure why this perplexed, panting officer is looking at all of them like they're in cahoots.

How does a boy vanish into thin air in a subway station? It's quite a riddle.

I can only live where there is light, but I die if the light shines on me. What am I?

A shadow.

One day, I think as I stand upright, the officer will figure it out.

From the small, shadowed space between two ticket machines, just a few feet away from the stairs that lead back to Eighty-Sixth Street, I step out into the dimly lit subway station and walk toward the light.

Twenty-Two

A group of teenage boys enters the station just as I leave. I stay as close to the handrail as possible to leave space between us. They are carrying duffel bags with lacrosse sticks over their shoulders. I keep my eyes to the ground, wondering if anyone will recognize me as the boy on the police horse.

Friday is tethered to a signpost and looks at me as soon as my foot hits the sidewalk. She snorts and flicks her tail.

"I'm sorry I got you mixed up in this too," I whisper. She blinks but doesn't look away. Crazy, but I feel like she didn't mind our ride, even though she's supposed to be on the police officer's side. Did she sense how much I needed her help? Did she know I needed to get away?

Shopkeepers and pedestrians are going about their regular business. Did they see me riding past them just a few minutes ago? I guess nothing can surprise New Yorkers. I keep my eyes on the concrete squares of sidewalk and plod onward, making my way back down from Eighty-Sixth Street to Seventy-Fourth Street. Max is surely at the hospital by now, but I still want to stay clear of the spot where I left her. Even an amateur lawbreaker like me knows not to return to the scene of the crime.

I wonder if the Amber Alert has gone off again—Max and I really have sent the city spinning. My mom would not be happy with what I've done, I think guiltily.

When I get to Eightieth Street, I turn right and walk back to the edge of the park. I see people, some carrying signs with messages about the marathon, but I don't see any runners here.

That's when I spot the enormous building to my right. It looks like some kind of royal palace with its arched entryways and tall columns, and I half expect a robed king and queen to step out along with armored knights. It stretches for blocks, and there are three tiers of stairs leading from the sidewalk to the heavy doors farther down from where I'm standing.

I wish Max were here with me. I climb the first set of steps and tell myself I can only sit for a moment. I put

Max's backpack next to me and think how lonely it looks without her.

I blink twice and my eyes focus in on a sign that reads *Metropolitan Museum of Art*.

There's another sign, a long vertical one that hangs like a drape between two columns. I read the letters stacked on one another like a word tower: *Vincent van Gogh*.

A young couple comes down the steps. They are each so busy with their cell phones that I think they'll probably walk into a wall. The guy crumples something up and tosses it at the trash can beside me. He misses—not surprising, since he barely looked up.

Auntie Seema would have tapped on his shoulder and made him pick it up. I figure I owe the city big time, and the least I can do is pick up this one piece of trash. Before I stand up to toss it into the bin, curiosity hits me and I uncrumple the ball. It's a brochure about a visiting van Gogh exhibit. I see the painting of a vase filled with sunflowers, some in full bloom and some wilting. Inside the brochure are more words and more paintings. On the back page, there's a painting of an outdoor café, tables and chairs set out on what looks to be a summer evening. The last painting is a dark sky filled with stars over a quiet village.

I read that van Gogh was Dutch and that he was born in 1853. He created more than two thousand pieces of artwork in the Postimpressionist style.

I read more and see that he was described as "troubled" and suffering from "mental illness." I wonder how a person with mental illness could also be "celebrated" and "gifted." Then I see a word I heard for the first time this weekend.

It has been suggested that Vincent van Gogh may have suffered from a form of epilepsy and that his disease may have led him to have the many visions . . .

That sounds an awful lot like what Max told me she has.

I wish I could show this to her. Did van Gogh need surgery too? I wish she could see this famous artist is just like her. Or she's just like him. They're just like each other. He wasn't normal. He was better than normal.

Auntie Seema might know. I stuff the brochure into Max's backpack.

I'm back on my feet. I feel more alone now than I did before I knew Max. So much has changed this weekend. I have to push on, though. The only hope I have of hearing from my mother is if I can get to Auntie Seema's home. Thinking of my aunt gives me the strength to put one foot in front of the other because I know that, even if she's not my mom, Auntie Seema will wrap her arms around me and make everything better.

I keep my eyes peeled for flashing lights, fleets of

runners, and blue-uniformed officers. I see only taxis, people of all ages, and sunlight glinting off windows. Nothing is out of the ordinary.

I hear the voices of a man and a woman behind me. By the way they sometimes break out with "Hey, there, chunky monkey," and "Did you make a stinky?" I can tell they're pushing a stroller with a baby in it. I listen to their conversation. They're talking about ordering Thai food for dinner and making the appointment for the baby's next set of vaccinations. I listen because as long as I know they're not talking about me, I'm invisible to them, and that's exactly what I need.

I make a turn and head into the park, taking a path that snakes through the trees and grass. The perfectly gridded streets of Manhattan disappear behind me. I have to keep my focus because I can't afford to get lost on this winding trail. I have to be sure I go straight across the park.

I've been ignoring a dark thought until now. It was easy to ignore it as long as Max was with me, but now that she's not, the thought is back. What will happen if I can't find Auntie Seema? Will I have to turn myself in? Will I be sent to foster care? If I asked them to send me to Afghanistan, would they? How will I find my mother there? Would we have to hide there? But they can't send me away since I'm an American. Could I sleep in the park or on the sidewalk like some of the people I've passed by?

Just get across the park, I tell myself. *You're almost there now.*

I've only been walking a few minutes when I hear it. It's the unmistakable roar of a crowd cheering. Then I see the banners and shouting friends and coolers full of sports drinks.

I sigh and walk up to the sidelines, slipping between people whose voices have started to go hoarse from cheering. Green paper cups crunch under my feet. There is no getting away from them.

How does a runaway kid cross a river of marathon runners without getting caught?

This is one riddle I don't have an answer for.

Twenty-Three

While I'm contemplating this new problem, I feel something vibrating against me. I look around, confused, until I realize it's coming from the backpack I'm wearing.

Max's phone! How had I forgotten? She must have turned it on and left it on.

I unzip the bag and feel around for the phone. My fingers touch something buzzing and I pull it out. I look at the screen and see a phone number with a 212 area code.

Should I answer it?

Before I can decide, the caller has hung up. I want to turn the phone off completely but I don't. I don't have Auntie Seema's phone number, and I don't dare try to call my mother again. There's no one I can call, but the phone still feels like a lifeline. I turn the ringer on because I might decide to pick up the phone if the number calls again. I slip it into the backpack and stare at the runners' path between me and the west side of Manhattan. Dr. Shabani is nowhere in sight. I wonder if she's still running or if she's already crossed the finish line.

The man next to me clears his throat and brings a shiny trumpet to his pursed lips. Where did he come from? He starts playing some kind of fight song and I can see the runners' faces lift, their arms pumping at their sides determinedly. I don't know what the song is but it seems to be telling them all: Don't you dare give up now.

I see a folding table stacked with towers of small green cups and a water cooler that's nearly as tall as me. There are three people standing by the table, filling cups and handing them to marathoners as they go by.

Mr. Fazio once told me that necessity is the mother of invention. It means that people start getting really smart when they need to—when there's something that's forcing them to think creatively. I really need to get across this path—the kind of need-to that should push me to have some brilliant idea.

The trumpeter plays on. He winks at me and waves his brassy horn around as he plays. His cheeks are red and puffed out like a chipmunk's.

Without interrupting his song, the trumpeter kicks the paper cups away from his feet. His fingers go up and down and up and down on the keys of the horn.

That's when necessity sparks a little idea.

I head to the table and smile widely at the women as I pick up a couple of green cups. I take a deep breath and remember how Max dove into the conversation with the man walking dogs. She was fearless.

"This is the best marathon, isn't it?" I say as one of the women looks over at me, bright eyed and cheerful.

"It sure is!" she says, beaming. "This is my fourth year volunteering here. Can't get enough of this!"

"So inspiring!" I say. I lean toward the barriers and reach into the running path. A woman in shorts and a tank top takes a cup from me. She huffs something that sounds like thanks. I pick up another green cup and smile back at the woman at the table. She's bopping up and down on the balls of her feet with excitement.

I squeeze through a gap between the barriers and hold the cups out to runners passing by. They disappear from my hands and I turn back to the table, reach over the barrier, and grab three more cups. I take a step farther into the running lane. After these three, I can see that there's an empty stretch of pavement before the next wave of runners. I'm in the middle of the path, my heart pounding.

"Here's some water. Way to go!" I yell.

"Hey, kid!" A volunteer from the table calls out to me. She's waving her arm around, beckoning for me to come back. "You can't be in there. Get out of their way!"

I look back at her and then raise my eyebrows.

I look around as if I hadn't realized where I was.

"Sorry!" I shout.

I dart behind the barriers on the opposite side of the course, getting out of the way just as a runner comes around the bend. I disappear into the folds of onlookers on the other side and speed walk away from the race.

Keep your cool, I tell myself. I'm not sure my maneuver was really a success. I start practicing my reply in case a hand lands on my shoulder. *I was just trying to help out.*

But I march onward, not running and not walking. No one approaches me, and I cross green lawns. I pass under the broad trees that cast shades like umbrellas. I ignore the growling in my stomach and pray that I'll be at the west border of Central Park soon. A family of geese walks past me. They look at me cautiously then veer off the asphalt path and back onto the grass.

I miss my mother.

I let my fingers graze a lamp post as I walk—the metal feels cool against my fingertips. Where is my mother now? It takes almost a day of flying to go from New York to Afghanistan. I was six years old when she told me just a little bit about leaving Afghanistan to come to the US. She was walking me to kindergarten on a rainy day.

How long did it take to fly from Afghanistan to America?

Well, when I leave my home it was Tuesday, and when I came to America it was Wednesday.

You were over the clouds for one day?

We had to stop to change planes once. But yes, for one day I was.

What was it like to be in the sky?

Peaceful. In Afghanistan, I saw what people do to the earth because everyone wants to say this is mine. They break it. Destroy it. And even when there is nothing left, they say mine-mine-mine. The sky is not like that. We cannot break the sky.

What did America look like from the sky?

My mother became quiet then, like she'd never been asked that question before.

Like something out of a dream.

A good dream?

My mother let her broken umbrella fall to her side then. She let the raindrops slide down her cheeks. My question went unanswered, carried away in a blustery moment.

I am thinking about that day when I realize I'm standing next to a stone wall. I look skyward and see the wall stretches into a tower, atop which flies a proud American flag. Ivy trails the sides of the tower the way melted ice cream oozes down the side of a cone.

I go up the steps and enter a stone castle. How have I stumbled upon a castle in the middle of New York City? I climb farther. I am on a high balcony, eye to eye with an oak tree. Tall, bright buildings loom over the treetops, but they are nowhere near this castle that seems to have fallen out of the sky and landed in the heart of this vast park.

I move deeper into the castle. It is empty of knights, empty of dragons, empty of swords and gauntlets. I look over the balcony's low wall. On the opposite side of the castle, there are moss-covered boulders.

"Max," I whisper, looking down at a deep and rocky drop-off. "You would love this."

My throat is dry. I see a spiral staircase, but I don't have the energy to walk to the top. I find a room with narrow windows in the stone walls and give myself permission to take a small break. It's even cooler in here without the sun's glow.

I sit with my back against the wall and feel the emptiness all around me.

"Look at your Shah, Mom. Here's your king sitting in a castle. Bet you never could have imagined this." Is this what it feels like to be a king? Did my father ever feel like a king? I have a growing list of questions I wish I could ask him.

It's dark in the castle, but there is a small window above my head. I know what my mother would say if she were here with me, looking at the opening in the stone wall.

I am that thing that falls on water without getting wet and falls to the earth without breaking. What am I?

"You are light," I whisper, missing my mother so much it hurts.

The soles of my sneakers are in bad shape. I'm no marathon runner, but I've surely put lots of miles on them today, I think. I open the backpack, wondering if there's any chance Max has forgotten some old granola bar or a few dollar bills. When I unzip the bag, I see Max's crumpled Statue of Liberty shirt.

"I can't believe you got away with that."

It feels better to talk with Max as if she's next to me. In a small way, it feels like she still is. I put the T-shirt on my lap and turn the bag upside down. Max's spiral-bound notebook with the striped cover and embossed *M* on the cover falls onto the ground and lands open. I don't move, remembering how Max wrote in that book as she sat hunched over it. Though I know I'm reading what she thought of as private, I lean in to see what she's written. I do it because I think this might be a way to hear her voice.

It's a letter to herself, neatly written words in black ink.

Dear Max,

There are a few things you should know about yourself—let's call them Max Facts. I'm writing this because I don't know what happens after brain surgery. I want ~~us~~ you to remember some important things, because if you forget these, you really won't be the Max I've worked so hard to become. I'm going to try to include everything that's important. I'll add to this whenever I can, but I just came up with this idea, and your surgery is three days away. I guess I've been hoping the surgery wouldn't really happen, and you wouldn't need this list. But I still haven't come up with a brilliant plan to avoid surgery so this is Plan B. Here goes:

1. Your favorite jeans are the dark-blue ones with the pink rhinestones on the back pocket.

2. You hate mushrooms. You've made it very clear that they are closer to shower mold than they are to real vegetables. After a year of arguments, Mom and Dad have finally accepted this. Do not lose this precious ground you've gained.

3. Get sesame seed bagels instead of poppy seeds. Way better and the sesame seeds don't get stuck in your teeth the way the poppy seeds do.

4. Brianna Kinsley stole your basketball in second grade. Actually, if you forget this it's all right.

*She's been pretty nice since then. I'll leave it on
this list though, because if anything else goes
missing, she should be high on the list of suspects.*

5. *Mrs. Roberts predicted you'd be a rocket scientist
because you are awesome at math and are in
general out of this world. You think this is a very
cool idea and have added Mars to the list of
places you want to visit.*

6. *Dad promised you an iPad for Christmas. Mom
rolled her eyes, so she may try to argue against
this, but a promise is a promise.*

7. *The nurse with the red hair calls you sweetie
because she can't remember your name. It's not
because she likes you that much. Please don't
wake up that naïve.*

8. *You hate having seizures. You hate the way they
make you feel just before and for a long time
after. You hate the doctor appointments and the
way people look at you and the way people do
anything they can to NOT look at you when they
find out about it. But it's not all bad. You know a
lot about the brain and medicines and tests and
hospitals, and you could probably be a really
good doctor if people with seizures are allowed to
be doctors. I doubt it. I don't even think they can*

drive, which is too bad. I think you'd look good in
a convertible.

I laugh, and my voice echoes against the cool stones of the castle. I'm sad that Max had to make this list, but think it was a brilliant idea to do it. The next page is written in blue ink. I'm surprised to see my name.

9. *Jason D is a cool guy. He's brave. That's actually*
   a word you hate but it fits him, and I can't think
   of anything else. Going alone to find his aunt
   when his mom's just been taken away is totally
   brave. Actually, if you're grounded forever when
   you're reading this and people say it's his fault,
   you should know that Jason D is only partly
   responsible for that. You decided to go with him
   when you heard his crazy-but-not-so-crazy plan.
   You should also know that as scary and hard
   as this day has been, you don't regret it for one
   minute. You're finally going to the zoo and you've
   got a new friend with an amazing story.

I remember Max taking her notebook out while we were sitting on the rocks by the pond. Is that when she wrote this about me? There's a lump in my throat. Max thinks I'm brave and I think I'm terrified. Which one of us is right? I don't know, but her words make me think I have a chance.

10. *You want a French bulldog. (Cats are not to be trusted. Ask Mom to tell you how you got the scar on your left forearm.)*
Please don't think this is everything. There are way more than ten important Max Facts, but now you're on the run and there isn't much time to write. Please try to hold on to the important stuff during the surgery. Please.

I close the notebook, missing Max even more. I hope that, whatever happens, she doesn't change one bit.

Twenty-Four

I hear voices approaching so I throw everything into Max's backpack and steal out of the castle, ignoring my hunger pains.

It doesn't take long before I reach the end of the park. I step onto the sidewalk and see cars streaming down yet another busy avenue. There's a man selling hot dogs out of a metal pushcart with a yellow-and-red umbrella. There are a few parked trucks behind him, the vehicles plastered with oversize menus. The sides facing the sidewalk have wide windows where people can place orders and pick up food. One truck has a picture of a great big taco on it. Another is painted in red, white, and blue stripes with *La Casita* written across the side, and a third has *Kebab*

Express in green block letters. They all smell delicious and make my mouth water, so I turn away.

Across the street, I see another huge building. It looks something like the art museum we saw on the east side of the park. This building has four soaring columns at the entrance and a statue of a man on a horse in front of it. There's a flag hanging from the light post on the curb.

American Museum of Natural History.

I know this museum. I haven't been inside, but my mom and I watched a movie once that showed all the exhibits of the museum coming to life at night. The movie was funny and, to be honest, I pulled out some of my old action figures and stood them on my dresser, right next to a picture of my father, before I went to bed that night. I wanted them all to come to life while I slept.

I walk in the direction I'm hoping will lead me back to Seventy-Fourth Street. I'm relieved to see a sign for Seventy-Seventh Street. At least I know I'm on the right track and just three blocks away from Auntie Seema's street. I keep my eyes straight ahead and cross three crosswalks without drawing much attention.

There's a kiosk on the corner of Seventy-Fourth Street. The man inside the booth is talking on the phone, a small wired earbud in his left ear. I eye the bags of chips and boxes of candy greedily. I would give just about anything for a bag of pretzels right now. I walk a little closer, as if hoping the man inside the booth will offer me a free snack.

As I inch my way over to the stand, a stack of newspapers catches my eye. I freeze when I see *AFGHANISTAN* in big bold letters splayed across the front page. I pick up the newspaper.

VIOLENT ATTACK IN AFGHANISTAN

My stomach drops. I read on. I skim the columns for words I recognize, for any clue about where my mother might be.

Kabul was battered by yet another brutal attack . . .

. . . warlords refuse to participate in peace talks . . .

. . . at least forty casualties . . .

. . . civilians rush to local hospitals to donate blood . . .

"This is no library."

The newspaper drops from my hands. I look up and see the man inside the booth staring at me with little patience.

"You want newspaper?" he says with a slight accent.

"Right, sorry," I say as I straighten the newspaper on the stack. If my mother is being sent to Afghanistan, she'll be sent to Kabul. That's where this front-page blast was. I walk away from the stand, trying not to picture the kind of explosion that would have killed forty people.

Once I turn down Seventy-Fourth Street, I look for Auntie Seema's building, my eyes scanning right and left down the block. I make it one block before I have to stop.

I am breathing hard and fast, and it feels like someone's hands are wrapped around my neck. I sit next to a pile of cardboard boxes.

Brutal attack . . . hospitals overwhelmed . . . donate blood.

How was my mother going to live in a place like that? I bury my face in my hands and groan.

The pile of cardboard boxes shifts, and I jump.

"What do you think you're doing here?" shouts an unshaven man with a camouflage jacket and filthy-looking cargo pants. A knit skull cap covers his head and forehead. "You can't just sit there!"

"I'm . . . I'm sorry . . ."

"You crying? Are you crying?" he asks, as if he can't believe his eyes.

"No!" I say quickly.

"No one out of diapers should be crying. That's what my momma used to tell me."

I nod, and wonder what will happen if I start walking away. I peek at the long cardboard box he just came out of and see a couple of plastic bags tied closed and a frayed green comforter. There's a coffee mug with a gold star on the side. In it are two pens, a toothbrush, and a pair of glasses. He's got a couple of newspapers in there too. I've seen people on the street asking for money before. My mom usually gives them whatever change she has in her pockets or a dollar.

It helps them a little. It helps us a lot, she always says.

"Yeah, it ain't much, but it's home," he says. I'm embarrassed that he's caught me staring.

"This is where you live?"

"Yeah," he says with a chuckle. He looks old enough to be someone's grandfather, but maybe that's just because I see gray hairs in his brown beard. "My piece of real estate."

I nod and look down the street, wanting to leave but not wanting this man to think it's because of him. He sees my fidgeting.

"Got somebody waiting for you?" he asks, his lips parted in a toothy grin.

"No. I mean, yes. My aunt, but she's not really waiting. She doesn't know I'm coming." I'm talking too much.

"That's the way to do it. Surprise them so they can't make up some story about having a doctor's appointment."

I smile politely.

"I don't think she would do that," I say.

"You don't, eh? Well, you're either right or you're wrong. How's that for wisdom? No charge for that one. And there's more where it came from too."

I've been told since I was old enough to walk that I'm not supposed to talk to strangers, and yet here I am. He lifts his head.

"Winter's gonna be brutal this year. We got off lucky last year."

I'm not scared away by this man. He hasn't asked me my name. He doesn't seem to care that I'm not with an adult.

"How can you tell?" I ask.

"Something . . ." He scrunches his nose up as if he's trying to catch a whiff of something. "Just something about the air. And I've seen lots of rings around the moon too. Something my grandfather taught me to do back home."

"I didn't think the moon had rings," I say.

He laughs.

"You never seen a ring of light around the moon? My granddad taught me to look for them when I was a kid. Sure way to tell what weather's coming around the corner."

"Where are you from?" I ask, trying to picture rings around the moon.

"Kansas," he announces, and clears his throat. He's got fingerless gloves on. "Ever been?"

"No. But I've heard of it."

"That's a start. Big, open skies that crack in half in thunderstorms. People with hearts as open as those skies."

"Why did you leave?"

I have my back against the building now.

"Joined the service."

I look back at the star on his cup and realize what it means.

"You were in the army?"

He nods. I remember that my father worked alongside American soldiers—like friends. It makes me want to talk to this man. I wonder if my father would be happy to see me with him.

"Stationed in a couple of places before I got sent to Panama."

"I don't know where Panama is," I admit. If he's disappointed that I don't know anything about where he's fought, he doesn't show it.

"It's a little paradise in Central America. Spent twenty-three ugly days there. I came home with a torn shoulder and one ear that can't hear anything quieter than a bullhorn," he explains, pointing to his left ear. "I was twenty-two years young then. Came back a month later feeling like an old man."

I don't know what I feel like, but I sure don't feel like a twelve-year-old kid today. I rub at my shins. They feel sore from all the walking I've done.

"There's a lot of war in Afghanistan too." I twirl the strap of Max's backpack around my wrist and pull so the strap presses into my skin.

"There's war everywhere. People can't live without it,"

he says, and chuckles again. There's a rasp to his voice that makes him sound tired but smart. "We always find a reason for war. Keeps us looking forward to peace, I suppose."

I can see he's been reading the same paper I spotted at the newsstand just around the corner. There's the headline about Afghanistan just a couple of feet from me.

"My mom's from there," I say, pointing to the newspaper. "Afghanistan."

"Hmph." He shifts his weight and arranges his legs so he's sitting cross-legged. "Bet she's glad she got outta there."

"She just got sent back," I say. As soon as the words come out, I wish I could unsay them. What if he figures out I'm alone? What if he reports me to the police? The man doesn't seem fazed, though.

"That's tough," he says slowly. "I have friends who served there. Nice people. Rough place. And now we've got a boy without his mother. That's bad news too."

There's no pity in his voice. He's just stating the facts. I'm glad for that. I'm ready to fall apart as it is. If he felt sorry for me, that might just tip me over.

"My father worked with American soldiers in Afghanistan. He was a translator."

"No kidding." There's a flash of wonder in his voice. "Can't do the job without some local friends."

I hear a crackling sound and a mechanical voice.

"Two-vehicle collision just outside Holland Tunnel outbound. No injuries."

"What's that?" I ask.

"That's my radio," the man says. He reaches into the box and pulls out a small black walkie-talkie. "I rigged this little thing here so I can catch police talk. Lot more interesting than anything else on the airwaves. And better than waiting for the news to hit the papers."

"You can hear everything the police are saying on that?"

He eyes me curiously, and I regret asking my question. I don't want him to think I've got reason to want to hear police talk.

"Not everything. Cuts in and out so I only catch some of the cross talk. That interesting to you?"

"Nah," I say, and shake my head. "Just never seen a walkie-talkie that could do that."

My stomach growls loudly, even more loudly than the walkie-talkie.

"Hungry, eh? I got some cheese crackers," he says casually. He pulls out five small packages of cheese and crackers, the kind that get packed into school lunches. "There's a guy that walks by here twice a week and drops off a bunch of these packages. Never anything else. Just these."

Those little packages look more precious than bricks of gold right now.

"I'm ... pretty hungry," I say. I'm also pretty embarrassed to be taking food from a man who lives in a cardboard box, but I haven't eaten anything since the sandwich Max and I shared.

"Wouldn't you know," the bearded man says with a lightness in his voice. "That those greedy-eyed city rats take one look at this stuff and walk right past."

I smile, surprised to hear his humor. It hits me that this man should be with his family. Why isn't he?

"Why didn't you go back to Kansas?" I ask.

He looks across the street and starts picking at his fingernails.

"I couldn't do it. I left Kansas a nice kid who'd never seen anything ugly. Most serious thing I'd ever done was put my little brother in a headlock. But then I got sent to Panama. Kid, once you've seen ugly, once you've been so close to ugly that it leaves its stink on you, you're not you anymore. I went back home and pretended to be that nice kid again. But I wasn't that kid, and I couldn't keep pretending. I didn't belong there anymore."

"But what about your family? Didn't they want you to stay?"

"I don't think so," he says. He lets his head hang low as

if he's embarrassed. "I think it was hard for them to have me around. Same for my old friends. I think they were all glad when I left."

I haven't known this man very long, but he seems like the kind of guy that people would like having around. I think he's pretty cool to talk with.

But what he said has gotten me thinking. Will I ever be the Jason D I was when I woke up Friday morning? Will I ever go back to Elkton? What would I say to Ms. Raz or Mr. Fazio in the laundromat? What would my teachers say if they heard about my mother? Would they not want me in the classroom?

"You ask some big questions for a little kid. What's your name?" he asks. His question feels like he's pressing on a bruise.

"Jason D," I reply.

"I'm Bartley."

"Sorry if I'm asking too many questions, Mr. Bartley."

Bartley shrugs, and turns up the collar of his jacket. "Better than not asking any."

I'm quiet for a moment but then turn back to him.

"If Kansas doesn't feel like home anymore, does New York City feel like home?"

"It should. It's home to everybody. New York's got rich people and poor people. Young people and old people. Koreans got their spot; Chinese got their part of town;

the Italians got a few blocks downtown; the Dominicans are a hundred blocks up from here; the Russians got their neighborhood in Brooklyn."

I hope there's a place for me here too.

"All of America in one little island," he says. "That's what New York City is."

It's hard to believe this place is an island. I haven't seen palm trees or sandy beaches. It's also hard to believe this place is little. The buildings are taller than any I've ever seen. Central Park seemed to go on forever. For a little place, everything is pretty big. And I'm trying to find one person on this island of millions.

I look back at Bartley. His mouth is pinched tight. He hangs on to his thoughts, swallows hard, and fidgets with the dial of the walkie-talkie. I notice his hands shake a little, and wonder if his family back in Kansas knows how he lives.

"I think your family must be really proud of you. And I bet they'd be really happy to see you again. Maybe they just didn't know what to say."

I think of Ms. Raz and the way she grumbled those first words of thanks when we started taking food to her. Bartley looks up at me. He scoffs at first and then runs his fingers through his hair.

"I bet they miss you."

His wet eyes glisten in the soft afternoon light.

"I was more scared of going back home than I was of being over in Panama," he says quietly. He pauses before he speaks again. "Maybe one day. Never say never, right?"

"I better get going," I say to Bartley. It's getting later. The sun's mostly hidden behind the buildings.

"Hang on, kid." He reaches into the cardboard box and pulls out the walkie-talkie. "Why don't you take this? I don't need it much anymore."

"Really?"

"Why not?" he asks. "When I was a kid, I used to think walkie-talkies were the coolest. Used my first set until it fell apart and I couldn't tape it back together anymore. Looks like you could use a little something to make your day better."

I take the walkie-talkie from him.

"Thanks, Bartley."

"It's good talking to you, little man," he calls out as I get back on my feet. He's staring at the ground. He exhales slowly, his cheeks puffed and round. "Really good talking to you."

I walk away from Bartley, Max's bag a little heavier with the weight of the walkie-talkie. I don't know why he gave it to me, but it makes me feel safer to have it.

I make it one block when something the bearded man said echoes in my head.

This can't be. How many hours have I spent getting here?

Auntie Seema told me she was just a block away from some great Dominican restaurants.

Everybody's got a home in New York City, Bartley said.

I sit on a fire hydrant. Bushy clouds have drifted across the sky and covered the sun's face. It is suddenly so cold that my fingertips go numb.

I lean over and hug my knees. I can't look up. Not right now. Not when I've just realized I've been going the wrong way.

Twenty-Five

I should have figured this out sooner. If I'd stopped to think, maybe I would have. Auntie Seema told me she lives around a bunch of Dominican restaurants. Bartley said that I was a hundred blocks away from the Dominican part of town. Auntie Seema doesn't live on Seventy-Fourth Street. She lives on 174th Street. The *1* must have gotten torn off with the tape on the return address label.

Could I be wrong? Not a chance. The buildings here look nothing like the ones I saw in the photograph, and there isn't a single Dominican restaurant for as far as I can see. I'm frustrated that I didn't put the clues together until now.

How am I going to travel one hundred blocks? I'm exhausted and hungry, and there's no denying now that my head's been throbbing. I touch the lump again. It's a reminder that things have been going wrong every step of the way.

I hear a click behind me and realize a door may be opening. I'm back on my feet and heading down the sidewalk as if I'm a block from home. I decide to return to the park. If I can follow the edge of the park north, I'll eventually get to 174th Street. It doesn't take that long to cross one block, I remind myself, so crossing one hundred streets is not impossible.

I pass Bartley's boxes though there's no sign of him, and I pass the corner kiosk with the newspapers. The museum is only a couple of blocks away, and the park is across the street. I walk along the shop windows and plan to cross the street at the next crosswalk.

On my left, there are fancy-looking apartment buildings with far more floors and windows than Ms. Raz's three-story structure. I keep my eyes on the pavement, glancing up often enough to be sure no one's looking at me strangely, and that I don't walk into a street sign. A few steps ahead there's a building with tall ground-floor windows giving a view of the lobby. I peek through the glass and see three people sitting in armchairs. There's a coffee table with magazines on it. A television is mounted on the wall, and I see a woman wearing a suit reporting the news from behind a desk. Something I see stops me dead in my tracks.

The news anchor is gone. On the screen is a school portrait, a blue backdrop with an American flag on one side.

The face in the middle of the portrait is mine.

It's my school picture that was taken at the start of school. I'm wearing a tan sweater. My face is curled into a broad smile. That picture was taken about a month before my mom told me she wasn't supposed to be in America. Then my portrait disappears, and a picture of the hospital is on the television screen.

I need a second to catch my breath. The hospital has somehow figured out who I am. They've also managed to get my school picture and broadcast it over the news. I am frozen. I've never seen my face on anything but my bathroom mirror. I never would have expected to see my face on a television screen in New York City! When I come to my senses, I look around to see if anyone noticed that I'm the boy on the television screen. Thankfully, no one's actually watching the news. They're all busy toying with their phones.

I stuff my hands in my pockets and keep walking, my head low. I wish I could disguise myself somehow, but

I don't even have a hat I can put on. I'm in front of the museum, where it seems easier to blend in because there are so many families here with plenty of kids around my age. I look across the street and see the food trucks lined up along the edge of the park. I should cross over now and disappear into the park. I'm in front of the wide steps that lead up to the museum when my backpack starts to ring.

It's Max's phone. I don't dare answer it.

"Hey, is that my phone?" Two women stand a couple of feet away from me. One of them, a young woman with short black hair and bright-red lipstick, opens her purse and starts digging through it. Max's phone continues to ring. I scramble to get the backpack off my shoulders. I need to turn this phone off now.

"You know, other people have phones too. It's not always yours," her friend teases.

"Ha!" the red-lipped woman shouts as she pulls a phone out of her handbag. "Found it."

The ringing doesn't stop because I haven't gotten Max's phone out of the bag yet. The moment I do, the ringing gets louder, and the two women turn around and look at me.

"Sorry," I say with a shrug, fumbling to reject the call. "I guess it was me."

It's the same number that called before. I surely won't answer it in the middle of the street with two women gawking at me. I stuff the phone into my pocket as casually as I can. I look up and see that the women are elbowing each other. The woman with the phone is nodding her head.

"Yup, that's totally him," she confirms.

"Are you sure?" her friend says, her voice rising with excitement. I feel my stomach do a flip. Do I run?

"C'mon now. You know I never mistake a face. That's *definitely* him."

"What do we do?"

They seem to be staring at me, their eyes out of focus, probably because they're wondering if I'm going to try to disappear again.

A woman with a yoga mat tucked under one arm stops and joins the other two ladies.

"Hey," she calls. "No way!"

My body comes back to life. I turn to my right to get across the street and run straight into the round belly of a man with a big camera pressed to one eye. I take two steps backward and the round eye of the camera is pointed at me.

"Get his picture, Daddy!" the two children at his side call out. "Get his picture!"

It looks like everyone's seen my face on TV. People are

222

staring, whispering to their friends, and some are even pointing. Since the moment I started running, I've been wondering when my luck was going to run out.

Now I know.

Twenty-Six

I put my hands up to cover my face, and hear a flurry of clicks.

"Don't be so obvious about it, Dad."

"Yeah, can you not look so paparazzi?"

"You guys are the ones who told me to get a picture! I don't even like his movies that much!"

His movies?

I look between my fingers and see that the camera is no longer pointed at me. It's pointed over my head. I turn and see a man in a light-gray blazer and white T-shirt. His jeans are dark and frayed at the hems. He's wearing sunglasses and a baseball cap as he walks his dog. If he's trying to be undercover, it's not working well. Even I recognize him.

I've watched him take down robots that invaded Earth. I've watched him catch a team of art thieves. I've watched him coach a hopeless Little League team through a turnaround season. It's slowly dawning on me that I'm not the object of everyone's attention. They're looking at Gavin Hopewell.

I'm looking at Gavin Hopewell.

Gavin's getting tugged by his impatient dog. He's signing autographs for a teenage girl, his hat hiding the expression on his face. Now I know what it means to be starstruck. I can't look away. In the science fiction movie, he had biceps as thick as fireplace logs and used them to swat off evil droids. He has the best lines and makes them sound even better because he has an Australian accent. The movie with the Little League team was my favorite, though. A bunch of kids from the wrong side of town couldn't afford uniforms or equipment with parents working two or three jobs. Gavin Hopewell played a coach who'd been fired from the major leagues so he was used to dealing with real athletes, not a bunch of kids. They could barely find first base when the movie started, but a hundred minutes later, they were sliding onto home plate like World Series winners.

Gavin did that for them. He turned them from losers into champs. In the final scene, Gavin was saying good-bye to one of the kids he had coached that season. He put his hand on the kid's shoulder, and the kid smiled at him. It was the kind of story that made everybody feel good because, in the end, who doesn't want a kid to win?

I remember that I have Max's phone in my pocket. I pull it out and flip it open. I press on the camera button and point it at Gavin. It's hard to catch more than his elbow because people have started to flock around him. I look around quickly and see that no one's looking at me. Why would they when a Hollywood star is a few feet away?

"Gavin, loved you in *Gripped*!"

"'The sun doesn't come up unless I tell it to,'" a boy yells, deepening his voice and doing his best Australian accent. It's one of those lines that stays with you long after the movie ends.

Gavin raises a hand and smiles. I move in closer. If I can ever get this phone back to Max, it would be really cool to have a picture of Gavin Hopewell on here for her. I slip between onlookers and keep the backpack close to me, trying to make myself as slim as possible. It works, and I find myself close enough to see that he has double-knotted his shoelaces. I have the phone's camera pointed at him. I click and snap a couple of pictures of Gavin talking.

They're blurry, though. I want to think it's because Gavin's moving around, but the truth is my hands are trembling.

"Brilliant day today. Good to see everyone out and about," he says cheerfully. He's not shouting, just talking loudly enough for the people around him to hear. He's acting like we all live in the same building and we've just bumped into one another in the hallway.

"That accent is delicious!" someone calls out, and laughter erupts. I turn around and see it's the woman with the yoga mat under her arm.

"As is yours, love," he says, and his mouth slips into a smile. It looks like he hasn't shaved in a couple of days. I notice that he's not as tall as he seems in the movies. People are staring, waiting for him to break into character or do something that they'll be able to post on Facebook tonight. He looks around and raises a brow. Then he leans over to scratch his dog's head. "Look at them, Rex. All these people have just run a marathon and all you do is walk."

There's more laughter.

"Right, right." He shrugs and gives Rex one last pat. I remember the dog that stole my backpack from me in Elkton. This one seems a whole lot friendlier but just to be certain, I check that Max's bag is securely on my shoulders. I've got to get a better picture but I don't want to look like I'm pestering him either.

"What about you? You a runner, mate?"

Gavin Hopewell is talking to me. I clear my throat and nod.

"I guess . . ." He's looking at me as if he really wants to hear my answer. A bit of truth escapes my lips. "I guess it depends on who's chasing me."

Gavin chuckles and taps his fist against my shoulder. He did the same thing as coach to the team's best player, a kid whose parents barely spoke English.

"Ah, you American kids are a clever bunch for sure!" he says brightly. "Are you a moviegoer?"

"For your movies, sure. You never let anything stop you," I say, forgetting that there's a ring of people around us. "I think that's why my friends and I like your movies so much."

Gavin takes his sunglasses off and hangs them on the collar of his shirt. He blinks twice. The corners of his eyes crinkle as he leans in and looks me directly in the eye.

"It's easy to be brave in front of the camera and on fake sets. Real life. Now that's a whole other story, isn't it?"

I nod.

"Real life is real hard," I say quietly. Why can't he become one of those heroes he plays in the movies and track down my mother and bring her back to me? I can picture it happening as if it's a movie I've already seen. My mother hugging me, both of us looking over at Gavin with gratitude as he walks away with a small tip of his cap.

He puts his hand on my shoulder and squeezes gently, his eyes falling on the phone I'm still clutching. He holds out a hand and raises one eyebrow. "Do you mind?"

I hand the phone over. Gavin steps over Rex's leash and stands beside me. He crouches down a bit and, with one hand, manages to snap a photograph of the two of us together. I can see both of us on the small screen. Gavin is smiling and my face looks like it doesn't know what to do. He hands the phone back to me and lifts a hand to the crowd, a simple farewell.

You American kids. That's what he'd said to me.

Do I look American to him? I suppose I look like the kids around me in class, but I'm not sure which of them are American either.

Gavin is walking away. People watch him disappear down the block. Rex looks much happier now that he's on his way, his fluffy tail wagging behind him.

"That was so cool!" A girl has come up to me. She's eyeing the phone in my hands and grinning. "He just snapped a selfie with you like you guys are BFFs or something! Wait, do you know him?"

I shake my head, and she says something else that I can't hear because my thoughts are too loud. I watch her

229

back as she walks away. I'm still wondering if I am an American. Sure, I was born in this country, but if my mom isn't supposed to be here, am I still American?

The cluster of people has melted away. I need to keep moving if I don't want to attract the wrong kind of attention. I see the food trucks still lined up on the park side of this avenue. I make my way to the crosswalk and join the handful of people waiting for the light to change.

The park is calling me. I want to disappear into it and let the trees and bushes hide me from the rest of the world. I walk past the food trucks and see that some are starting to shut down. I have just ducked between the trees when the walkie-talkie crackles loudly.

"Amber Alert child spotted on Seventy-Fourth speaking to homeless man by someone living in the neighborhood. Any units in the vicinity, let's get out there and ask some questions."

I press my back against a tree, wishing its trunk were a hollow I could hide in. My breathing is quick. Real life is scarier than any movie I've ever seen and all the movies my mother never let me see.

I look around and see nothing but empty fields and long walking paths. I'll be out in the open no matter which way I go. I look up at the afternoon sky. There's a full, white moon, so pale it looks like I can see through it. Clumps of clouds are scattered about. Nighttime will be here soon too, which makes me nervous. What am I going to do?

They're closing in on me, I think, remembering my school photograph on the television screen. They're on my trail, and it's getting harder and harder to hide.

Twenty-Seven

I come back to the park's edge. I need to see if there are any lights and sirens approaching. Are they really going to question Bartley? He's only going to tell them things they already know. I'm glad I didn't figure out I needed to get to 174th Street before I left him. He can't share what he doesn't know.

I'm a few blocks north of Seventy-Fourth Street, but that's not very far, and I imagine the police will start to search the area once they get through Seventy-Fourth Street. Do I dare try to get back into the subway? That would be the quickest way to move through town, but it's risky because I have to find a subway station, and I don't know where the nearest one is.

I duck behind an elm tree and crouch to the ground. I'm mostly hidden by a round, green trash can. A scraping sound comes from inside the trash can, something scratching against the metal container.

Two of the food trucks are still there, but the kebab truck is gone. There's a man shutting the window of the taco truck. He waves at the brown-haired woman by the La Casita truck that is striped in red, white, and blue. She waves back and watches from the sidewalk as he slides into the driver's seat and pulls his door shut.

She's wearing jeans and a quilted blue jacket, the same shade of blue that covers a third of her truck. She is picking up the napkins and plastic forks people have dropped just outside her vehicle and putting them into a plastic bag. That's when the passenger-side door of the truck opens and a girl steps out.

"Mami, let me help," she calls as she reaches to take the bag from her mother's hands.

"It's okay, *amor*. Just work on your homework. That's more important. I can finish here."

There's something warm and familiar about this woman. She reminds me of my mother even though they look nothing alike. Like my mom, she's got a light accent, though hers sounds very different.

Her daughter, a girl with straight black hair and dark eyes, tucks a pen behind her ear and takes the bag from her mother.

"You can take care of the food inside. It'll be faster this way."

Her mother kisses the top of her head as a sign of agreement. The woman goes into the truck through a door in the back and closes the panel of the serving window. The girl picks up a few more napkins and a paper cup. When she's satisfied that there's no other litter to collect, she walks over to the garbage can just a few feet away from me.

As she gets closer, I can see that she's probably still in elementary school. She's got tiny, gold hoop earrings and a puffy, pink jacket on. I try to look away so she won't think I'm spying on her, but as I do that, the walkie-talkie crackles with static. She turns sharply around and spots me by the tree.

"Oh! I didn't see you."

I give her a quick smile, get to my feet, and dust off my pants. "Sorry, didn't mean to surprise you."

She nods, and I watch as she tries to put the bag of collected trash into the waste bin. The trash can is full, so she pushes the bag into the pile with two hands.

Just as she's pulling her hands away, there's a rattling and rustling inside the trash can.

"What is tha—!" she exclaims.

That's when a gray squirrel leaps out of the trash like a firecracker on the Fourth of July. Unbelievably, he lands on her shoulder. She lets out a scream, and the squirrel bounces onto the sidewalk. His tiny legs moving so fast that they're a blur, he vanishes into the greenery of the park.

I'm at her side in a second. She stumbles backward and her foot catches on a bicycle rack. I manage to catch her just as she's teetering toward me. Together, we topple over, but I've braced her fall.

"Are you okay?" I ask her. For a second, I've forgotten about wanting to stay hidden.

She touches her hand to her ankle and laughs nervously.

"I am. Are *you* okay?" she asks, looking at me to see if I've got any injuries. I don't. I've landed on my hip but barely scraped my palms on the concrete.

"I'm fine. That was some crazy squirrel, huh?" I say, and get to my feet.

"Liz!" a voice hollers. I turn to see the passenger-side door of the truck open. The woman in the blue jacket rushes out to get to her daughter. "Did I just see a squirrel on your shoulder?"

"It's okay, Mami!" she says, though she's still on the ground. "I think I scared the squirrel too!"

"Are you sure you're okay?" Her mother looks worried.

"Oof, I think so." She scrambles to her feet, and I hold my arm out. She smiles as she uses it to rise.

"Thanks!"

"Sure," I say quietly.

"I've never been hit by a flying squirrel," she says with her hands on her hips. Her mother is at her side now, her brown eyes warm with concern. She's looking her daughter over to be sure she's really okay.

"Where did that come from?" her mother asks. Again, she reminds me of my mom. Maybe it's the soft lines on her face. Maybe it's the way she smiles or the way she touches her daughter's head. Then she turns to me.

"And what a gentleman you are!" she says.

"No big deal," I say with a shrug.

"Unbelievable," the woman says, shaking her head. She looks at me through narrowed eyes, the kind of look a mother gives when she's figured something out. "You were nice to help. Are you hungry? I have some spinach-and-cheese empanadas in the truck—still warm."

"They're really good," says her daughter with a nod.

The woman beckons me to follow her with a wave. She climbs in through the back door and hands me two empanadas, warm as promised, wrapped in wax paper. The cheese crackers didn't do much to curb my hunger, so these smell really good right now.

"Where's your mother or father? I want to tell them they should be proud of you, coming to help a young girl." She's looking around, waiting for an adult to appear and claim me.

"My mom's around here somewhere," I say, trying to sound believable. "She'll probably be by any second now."

"You're not here alone, are you?" the woman asks. Her face has turned serious.

"No, no. I'm here with her and a bunch of other people."

A bunch of other people? Why would I say that?

"Oh, okay," she says, unconvinced. She's still looking around for all the people I'm with.

"I'm . . . uh . . . I'm here filming a movie," I say. I would kick myself if it wouldn't make this moment worse. "With Gavin Hopewell. Do you know him?"

"I know him!" shouts Liz. "He's my brother's favorite movie star."

Liz's mother squints a little. She's either not buying my story or she's got a massive headache. It's also possible that my story is giving her a massive headache.

"Yeah, I'm just taking a break from the filming. We're shooting in the museum, actually. Lots of cameras and lights . . . and . . . and . . . and . . . action," I say, fumbling for words.

I see Liz's mom has her mouth half-open. She's about to poke a hole in my story, so I grab Max's phone out of the backpack.

"I wouldn't normally share this, but here's a picture we just took together." I click on the photo gallery and pull up the last picture taken, the selfie Gavin snapped with me across the street. I show Liz, and her mother peers over her shoulder.

"Wow!" exclaims Liz.

I slide the phone back into the backpack.

I see her mother's forehead relax. She almost looks impressed, actually.

"Yeah, so we've still got a bunch of work to do in there, and I better get back." I point to the museum with my left hand while the empanada warms the fingers of my right hand.

"See that, Liz? You've met a real movie star today! But we better get going. I don't want to get home too late," she says with a sigh. She points her daughter to the truck.

"So cool," Liz says excitedly. "I can't wait to tell Marlon."

I take a bite of the empanada and have to fight the urge to run up and hug this kind woman. It is warm and cheesy and just what I needed. Liz walks to the passenger-side door while her mother walks around the front of the truck to the driver's side. As my eyes follow her, they fall upon the black lettering on the door of the truck.

La Casita
215 177th Street, #201
New York, NY

That's three blocks away from Auntie Seema's apartment. Could it be that this truck is headed there now?

My heart starts to race again. Liz is looking at me curiously.

"Are you sure your mom is around here?" she asks.

"Yeah, yeah. She just stepped away to say hi to a friend," I say, debating if I dare ask for a ride. How am I going to explain where I'm going? "Are you . . . are you going to 177th Street?"

"Yeah, why?"

"Just . . . just curious."

I stuff the rest of the empanada in my mouth, partly because I'm hungry, but also because I want to stop myself from saying anything else. Liz reaches for the handle of the door then stops short.

"You look a little . . . a little nervous or something."

"Me? Nah!" I say, and wave her suggestion off as if it's ridiculous. Meanwhile, I'm wondering if I'd be able to grab on to the back of this truck and hitch a ride. "Just a little tired from all the . . . acting I've been doing today."

She nods, accepting my answer in that way kids do.

"All right. See you."

I hear the truck's engine start and a lump grows in my throat. That's when I notice that the back of the truck is half open. Liz's mother forgot to close it. I move toward the truck to close it for them and peek inside. On the right side is the window that opens to customers. It's closed, but I can see the handle to open it. There are shelves beneath the window with stacks of paper bags and small cardboard boxes. On the left side of the truck is a kitchen. There's a long grill and a stovetop. There's even a sink. It really is a kitchen on wheels. I can see straight through to the front of the truck and the two seats where Liz and her mom are sitting. Neither of them has noticed that I'm standing at the back of the truck or that the rear door is open.

I'm not the bravest kid in the world, but maybe, just maybe, I can act like I am. I slip one foot onto the back of the truck, just to see what it would feel like.

That's when I hear sirens.

Twenty-Eight

My heart leaps into my throat, and I move without thinking. I step into the back of the truck as quietly as I can and crouch low as I pull the door closed behind me. I don't slam it shut, but pull it hard enough that it makes a soft click. The noise is hard to hear, though. Police sirens are wailing so loudly that they must be just outside the truck.

"What's going on here?" I hear Liz's mom ask. Is she talking to me? I hold my breath and wait.

"No clue. Did you do something you're not telling me?" Liz asks playfully. Her mother starts to laugh.

"Ha, ha, ha," she says sarcastically, and I feel the truck shift gears and lurch forward.

I press my back to the stainless steel cabinets and inch inward until I can duck into the hollow space beneath the grill.

"Three police cars. Something's got them excited."

That reminds me that I need to do something. I unzip Max's backpack and take out the walkie-talkie and the phone. I mute the phone and flick a switch on the side of the walkie-talkie to *OFF* to be sure nothing crackles to life or starts ringing to give me away.

"Hey, Mom, do you think that kid was okay?"

I freeze.

"I hope so. Why, did he say something to you?"

"No. But he looked like he wanted to say something."

The radio comes on. Spanish lyrics fill the car. I hear trumpets and drums and a man's voice singing. Every few minutes, I am bounced off the floor so hard that I wonder if this truck has run over a small car. How long will it take to get me to 174th Street?

The truck is stopped, probably because of a red light. I'm panicked, though, thinking that at any moment Liz or her mother will turn around and see my sneakers or my elbows and call the police on me for sneaking into their truck.

There are no windows, so I can't see how close we are to 177th Street. My plan, which is not much of a plan, is to jump out the back door once they park the car. Then

I'll have to run and hide, because they're sure to be angry that I've hidden myself in their truck.

The truck starts moving again. This time it pulls forward with a bigger lurch.

"Agh, my math book," Liz exclaims. Her textbook has fallen in the open space between the driver and passenger seats. She reaches over to retrieve it. I hold my breath and try to pull my toes and knees closer to me and out of sight.

"Oh!" Liz says sharply.

"What's the matter?" her mother asks.

My palms get sweaty. I can't make myself any smaller.

"Um, nothing. Nothing. Just grabbing my book."

"Did you finish your homework?"

"I did," Liz says slowly.

I poke my head forward, just enough to spot Liz looking over the armrest of her seat. Our eyes meet and I pull my head back quickly.

Now what?

My breathing quickens, and I wait to see what Liz is going to do about me sneaking into their truck.

"Liz, are you okay? You look like you've just seen a ghost."

"Nope," Liz replies. "No ghost."

"I should hope not," her mother mutters. "We're going to stop by your *tía's* house to drop off some of the food left over from today. I don't want it to go to waste."

"Sure, of course not," Liz says. Her voice is high-pitched and musical—more than a little suspicious. If Max were here, she would not be impressed. Then again, Liz is probably not used to hiding a stowaway from her mom. This probably doesn't come naturally to her.

The truck slows to a stop and Liz's mother turns the engine off.

"All right, here we are. I'm going to run in and drop off that tray of food. Don't open the door to anyone, got it?"

I hear the unclicking of a seat belt and a door opens.

The tray of food.

In a second, that back door is going to swing open and I'll have no choice but to leap past Liz' s mother and make a run for it. My mother would be terrified and angry at the things I'm doing today, but how else am I going to keep myself out of foster care or jail?

"Mami, let me get that tray for you!"

In a flash, Liz has unbuckled herself from her seat and bounded past me. She's so fast that she could have put that squirrel to shame. She doesn't say a word to me, but climbs over the divider into the back. She shoots me a strange look, grabs a plastic bag holding an aluminum tray, and reaches the back door just as her mother cracks it open.

"Here you go!" Liz sings.

Her mother is silent. I hear the crinkle of plastic and

know she's taken the bag from her daughter's hands.

"Liz, you're going to bed early tonight. You're not acting like yourself, and I'm worried about you."

"Just trying to be helpful," Liz explains, her voice bright and cheery. She's got her hand on the door handle, ready to pull it closed and not allow her mother to open it any wider. The door closes with a loud click and Liz turns around to face me.

"What are you doing in here?" she whispers.

"Thanks for not telling on me," I say. "I don't know why you did that."

There's something about the way she's looking at me, her head tilted to the side and her eyes demanding answers, that reminds me of Max.

"I could tell you were in trouble. I've seen that same look on my brother's face a million times. And if my brother were here, he would tell you that you can't hide from my mom for too long. What are you doing in here? Are you running away from home?"

Yes, I want to tell her, but only because it's not home anymore.

"I'm trying to get to my aunt's house. She lives on 174th Street."

"Where are your parents?" she asks.

"Not here." I don't want to get into the details with Liz. Sure, she didn't tell her mother that I'd snuck onto their truck, but how do I know I can trust her? What if she tells her mom everything as soon as she gets back?

"Maybe this is a bad idea," she says slowly. "Maybe you should leave."

"Look, I only have my mom and she's just been sent back to her country. I have nowhere else to go but to my aunt's house."

"Oh," she says. Her reaction is quiet and contained. "You're alone?"

"Yeah." I nod.

"Aren't you scared?"

"Doesn't matter if I am. I've got to keep going."

Gavin Hopewell would be proud if he could hear me.

"Where's your mom's country?"

I can see that Liz is softening toward me. She's not going to kick me out of the truck or report me to her mother.

"Afghanistan."

"So you're Af-ghan-i-stani?" she asks, struggling with the syllables.

"Afghan. And no. My mom is Afghan."

"Then so are you."

"No, I'm American." I have to be. How else can I explain why my mother goes and I stay?

"My parents are from Dominican Republic. I'm Dominican and American. You can be both, you know."

Being Afghan didn't seem to help my mother very much. I don't see how it'll help me.

"Right now, I need to get to my aunt's house."

"You said 174th Street, right? That's not far from where we live," Liz says thoughtfully.

"Where are we now?" I want to get up and take a look out the windshield, but I'm afraid Liz's mother is on her way back and will spy my face in the window.

"This is Ninety-Seventh Street. We're still a long way from home."

We are both quiet. Liz glances out the window.

"She's coming!" she says in a hush. She looks back at me and then over to the back door.

"I should go," I say, even as my heart breaks to think how far I'll still have to travel on my own. I get to my feet and slip the backpack onto my shoulders. Liz purses her lips, then folds her arms across her chest.

"And get me in trouble for hiding you?" she says in a loud whisper. "No, thanks! Just stay where you are!"

"But what about—" I protest.

"I don't know. Shoot, she's coming!" she says, stumbling her way back into her seat and fastening her seat belt. I go back under the grill, pressed against the side of the truck. I can hear Liz muttering nervously. "Man, Afghans are just as stubborn as Dominicans."

Twenty-Nine

"Your aunt's got the flu or something. She was wearing a red-and-white bathrobe and socks. Big white socks that go up to her knees. She looks like Santa Claus on his day off. You wouldn't like it, *mija*."

Liz laughs, a small and nervous chuckle.

"A red-and-white bathrobe? That's pretty funny."

Her mother pauses for a second.

"Are you sure you're okay? If you're stressed out about the math test, you're going to do just fine. You've been studying hard, and you have two more days before the exam."

"I guess you're right, Mami. I've just got to believe that everything will be fine," she says, and I feel my chest relax.

The truck is back in motion and headed to 177th Street. This is as close as I've been to Auntie Seema's home, but I wonder if I'm going to be disappointed again. Is it possible she's moved? Maybe that's not her address anymore. I push the thought aside and open Max's backpack and pull out the notebook. Do I dare read more of her private thoughts? When I was in the castle, the book flipped open without my help. This time, I lift the cover on purpose. I really want to hear Max's voice.

The middle of the notebook is where Max started writing her list of things to remember about herself after the surgery. I turn the pages slowly, doing my best not to attract attention with the rustling sound of pages turning. Max's handwriting now looks familiar to me. I can hear her voice as I read her writing. I open to the beginning of the notebook. There are two blank pages and then Max's handwriting appears.

One of these days, I'm going to get a passport and fly all around the world. I'm going to hop from one country to another, and try to learn lots of new words along the way. Dad brought home a container of gelato yesterday. (That's ice cream from Italy.) It was the most amazing chocolate thing I've ever had, and I've had a lot of chocolate. So, I have this idea for my tour around the world. Everywhere I go, I'll stop and taste the ice cream. I'm going to write a book about all the different kinds of ice cream, and then share my reviews with people who are wondering what ice cream in South Africa tastes like.

I hope that I'll be able to fly around the world. Right now, my mom gets nervous when I go into the backyard alone. Epilepsy is with me everywhere I go. Every time my mom fills out a camp form or RSVPs for a birthday party, someone's got to find out that Max is epileptic. I don't want to be an epileptic. I just want to be Max. Maybe even Max who sometimes has seizures. But mostly just Max.

I wish I could talk to Max. I wish I could tell her that she's not just an epileptic. She's way more than that. I don't know if I'll ever get this notebook back to her, but I reach into the bag and pull out a pencil with tiny bite marks in the wood. I can picture Max nervously chewing on the eraser end.

The road is getting a little rougher, and I do my best to stay tucked into the small space under the grill. Liz and her mother are talking quietly, and the radio is turned up so I can't make out what they're saying.

I flip to a blank page and hold the pencil, its tip bouncing on and off the paper as the truck jostles us about. I start to write. My thoughts are as messy and jumbled as my handwriting.

Max—I'm sorry I looked in your notebook. Please don't be mad. You're a riddle that I can't seem to figure out. That's what makes you fun to hang out with. I never would have gotten as far as I did without you. I'd probably still be in the hospital. If you can break out of a locked hospital floor, you can definitely make it around the world. I just hope you'll find your way home after you do because I will try to find you. You're a really cool friend.

I close the book and slip it back into the backpack. Slowly, so that it doesn't make much noise, I zip the bag shut and hold it against my legs. Just as I'm wondering how far the truck has driven, I hear Liz's voice over the music.

"Hey, we're on 169th Street already? Mami, you're driving fast today!"

"Liz, with all this traffic . . . you think I'm speeding? You could walk faster than I'm driving."

Liz swings her head around. She and I make eye contact for a split second and I nod, thanking her for the secret update. We're getting really close now, and I've got to come up with my exit plan. I've got only eight blocks left before they stop the truck.

I think about what Liz said and wonder if it's possible to be two things. Can I be American and Afghan? I may not have been born in that country, but I'm hiding in a truck right now because of what happened there. The food I eat is Afghan, the music we listen to is Afghan, the gift-filled holiday I look forward to is Eid, not Christmas or Hanukkah.

But I'm American too. I watch NBA games and Thanksgiving Day parades. My favorite foods are macaroni and cheese and chocolate chip cookies. I cheer for the US team during the Olympics. I can understand a few words in Dari, but I only really speak English. Don't those things make me American?

Just as I'm debating what I am, the truck slows down. It inches back and forth a few times and finally comes to a full stop.

"It's supposed to get cold tomorrow," Liz's mother reports. "Winter's finally going to be here, and I think it's going to be a bad one. I can feel it in my bones."

I try to curl myself into a tight ball and hold my breath so I don't make a sound. I hear the truck doors open and, after a moment, close again.

"You need some new sweaters, Liz."

"Dad said he would take me shopping next weekend."

From the distant sound of Liz's voice, I can tell they are out of the vehicle but still close by. I take a small breath. I wait a few moments and hear their voices fade. Once I hear nothing but cars rolling past, I slowly come out from under the grill. I move one limb at a time and crawl on all fours to the front of the truck. From there, I poke my head up like a periscope coming out of the water, to see if Liz or her mother are anywhere in sight. I see a few people walking around with jackets buttoned up to their chins. The temperature has dropped since earlier this afternoon, and the sun is hidden behind the buildings.

I check Max's backpack again, making sure all the pockets are zipped tightly. I check the laces of my sneakers. I do all these things because I'm a little nervous to step out of this truck. This is when I find out if I've correctly solved the riddle of where Auntie Seema lives. The next puzzle is how Auntie Seema can get me back to my mom in Afghanistan.

That's what I've decided today—that I won't be home unless I'm with my mother. If that means living in Afghanistan, then that's where I'll go. If it's dangerous there, then I can't let my mom face that alone. I don't think my dad would want that for her, knowing the kind of guy he was. I'll be an American living in Afghanistan. Here, I'm an Afghan-American. If I lived in Afghanistan would I be an American-Afghan? It doesn't really matter what people want to call me. At the end of the day, I'm Jason D, the kid named after the second half of the year.

I move to the back of the truck. I can unlock that door and slip out onto the street. What if someone spots me coming out of here? I practice what I'm going to say, my hand on the door handle. *I was just cleaning up a few things for my aunt. We sold lots of empanadas today!* And then I'll walk away as calmly as I can. I won't smile too widely. I won't whistle. I won't run. That is my plan.

I take a deep breath and press down on the door handle. I hear a click and swing the door open, daylight flooding the back of the truck. The sun is not completely gone yet. The truck is parked along a sidewalk, with a car a few feet behind it. I step out and see two men walking away from me, their backs turned so they don't notice that I've just climbed out of La Casita.

I close the door behind me, my heart thumping loud and hard and steady like a drum. My hands are cold, even though I'm sweating. I walk around the truck to the sidewalk to figure out what street I'm on and which way I need to go to get to 174th Street. I'm standing next to the truck, straining my eyes to spot one of those green street signs on the corner. I want to jump for joy when I see that I'm on 175th Street. I'm just a block away from Auntie Seema. I could almost celebrate, but then a voice breaks through my happy thoughts.

"Did you just climb out of my truck?"

The drum in my chest beats harder. I spin around and see Liz's mom, her hands on her hips, and the expression on her face not a happy one at all. The line I rehearsed in the truck is not going to work on her.

"I was . . . I just . . . I didn't mean to . . ."

She takes a step closer to me, and that's when I see Liz pop around the corner.

"Wait, Mami, I'll get your phone—" Liz is shouting. She stops abruptly when she sees that her mother and I are face-to-face, a few squares of concrete sidewalk separating us.

"You didn't mean to sneak into my truck? Where are your parents? Why are you lying?"

She's right. I am lying, and that makes me a liar. A liar. A sneak. I think of all the things I've done since I left my house. My face turns bright red with all the shame I've kept bottled until now. Liz looks stuck, like she can't figure out what to do so she does nothing.

"I'm sorry," I shout, my voice about to crack. "I really am. I won't bother you again."

I turn to walk away, hoping she'll just let me leave. I want to run, but I also know that'll make me look and feel like a real criminal.

"Get back here! You can't just leave! I'm going to call the police."

"Mami, don't!" Liz cries out.

I turn to look over my shoulder and see Liz's mother reaching for the truck's door. In a second, she's pulled out her cell phone—that's what she must have come back for—and is yelling again. I have no choice. I start to run. She's not chasing after me, but I need to get away.

"I'm calling the police right now!" she shouts. Liz is at her side, biting her lip and looking pained. That's when Liz's eyes go wide with fear. She points in my direction, her finger jabbing at the air with some kind of urgent message.

"Officer!" Liz's mom calls out.

I whip my head around just in time to see, one block away, a cloud of blue, a flash of gold, and a surprisingly familiar face.

"Jason D!" yells Officer Khan.

That's when I run.

Thirty

I can hear shouting behind me, but I don't turn back. There's no talking my way out of this situation. It's not like the time I galloped off on Friday. This time the whole world has come crashing down, and I'm running for my life.

The backpack is slapping against my body as I run. It's slowing me down, and I can't afford to be slowed down a single beat, so I wiggle my way out of the straps and let the backpack fall to the ground. I'm faster without the bag on my back but it hurts to have to let it go too.

I turn at every corner, hoping to confuse Officer Khan and lose him along the way. I turn around and see him shouting something at me, but there's a solid block between us, and my ears are buzzing so I can't hear what he's saying.

I pass an older woman with her hair wrapped in a scarf. I pass two toddlers tugging on their mothers' arms. I pass a man leaning against a storefront drinking a bottle of juice. If they are giving me curious looks, I don't notice it because I'm trying to figure out my next move.

I turn left again, my chest burning because I'm running my hardest. I'm running past buildings of tan bricks, five stories high with black fire escapes and windows with bars. I pass by a store called *Farmacia* and another called Gourmet Deli. I make a right. There's a redbrick building, music blaring from one of the ground-floor windows. There's a church with a narrow steeple and stained-glass windows.

I make another right.

How much farther can I go? I turn around and don't see Officer Khan or Liz's mother. The buildings here are of different heights, some taller and some shorter. There's nowhere to hide on these streets, no small alleys to duck into. I see a moving truck with its back door wide open. It's parked in front of a tan building with the number 345 in white scrolled numbers on the glass door entrance. Just outside the entrance are a few big pieces of furniture wrapped in fabric. One looks like a kitchen table. Another is almost certainly a sofa.

I look around. The block is empty. My eyes scan upward to the fire escapes. Some are bare, but others are like small gardens with pots of green-leafed plants and some flowers.

My brain races, calculating the possibility. Can I do this? I have to try. The table is positioned right under the ladder of a fire escape. I quickly hop onto it, hearing voices echoing in the lobby of the building. I jump up, my fingers making contact with the last rung of the fire escape, but I don't have enough of a grip. I slip back down to the table and land with a thud.

"Come on," I mutter, glancing up at a rung that looks painfully close. I make another leap and fail again, my fingers slipping once more.

"One more try," I say through gritted teeth. This time, I manage to hang on with my right hand. I dangle for a couple of seconds, then get my left hand to hook on as well. With a grunt, I swing my legs up and tuck them close to my chest. The soles of my sneakers catch onto the bottom rung and I hang there like a caterpillar curled on a twig.

The voices from the lobby get closer, and I hear a police siren in the distance. I push off with my feet and start to climb, one rung at a time, hand over hand, until I reach the first landing. I look down just in time to see two men come out of the building. They're wearing yellow T-shirts that match the logo on the truck with the open back.

"Let's grab that sofa first," says one of the guys.

I have my back against the bricks of the building, in a narrow space between two windows, in case anyone inside happens to look out. The movers, one at each end of the covered couch, disappear into the lobby. As soon as they do, I scramble up the ladder and onto the next landing on the fire escape. This one's got a long narrow planter with chili pepper plants. I tuck myself between the two windows of this third-story landing and look down. There's a long way to go from here to the sidewalk.

Officer Khan comes running around the corner, looking left and right and panting. The movers are back on the sidewalk, looking at him curiously.

"Hey!" he shouts at them. "You guys!"

"We've just got this last piece to get in there and we'll move the truck. Cool, officer?"

"Have you seen a kid run past here?" Officer Khan puts a hand against the middle of his chest. "He's about this tall, wearing jeans and a green polo shirt."

"Nah, but we've been in and out of the building. Sorry, can't help ya."

There's a loud ring, and Officer Khan pulls his cell phone off a clip on his belt and presses it to his ear.

"Yeah?" he says breathlessly. "I'm on 174th. He's got to be somewhere around here."

174th Street? Somehow in my many left and right

turns, I've wound up on Auntie Seema's street. I try to stay calm.

"How far away are you?" Officer Khan asks. He's pacing in front of the building's entrance. Any second now, he's going to look up and see me staring down at him. I get up slowly, careful not to make the fire escape rattle and clang with my movement.

I climb up the ladder to the next landing, as stealthy and nimble as Max was when she picked up the nurse's badge and freed us from the locked unit. Once on the fourth floor, I look down again and see Officer Khan still pacing, still with the phone pressed to his ear. It's harder to hear what he's saying from here. There's a rolled-up carpet in the corner of the landing along with a small potted geranium.

I have an idea and grab the carpet, doing my best to carry it under one arm as I make my way up to the last landing on the fifth story of the building.

When I arrange the carpet the way I want it, I can breathe a little easier. That's when I hear the movers back on the sidewalk.

"I told you we'd be done before five. Dinner's on you, brother."

"You got it. I saw a hot dog cart down the street."

"Man, did you get up on this table? Look at these footprints."

"Why is everything my fault?"

Their voices are getting louder.

"Not everything's your fault. Just the stuff you do! And why are you so defensive, dude? If this is about the hot dog . . ."

"What in the world are you guys arguing about?" That's Officer Khan's voice. I know it well by now. I hold myself as still as a statue and wait to see if they will figure out that the footprints lead to a boy hiding on the fire escape.

Thirty-One

"Nothing. Nothing," says one of the movers. He sounds grumpy.

I watch Officer Khan move farther down the block. He looks like he's waiting for someone.

"Seriously," says one of the movers. "Why are there footprints on this table?"

If the movers have bothered to look upward, I can't tell, because as soon as I got to this landing, I unspooled the carpet, using it to make a solid floor on the fire escape. Anyone looking straight up won't be able to see me. I'm still visible, though, to anyone looking this way from down the block.

"I don't know, maybe you stepped on the cover before you put it on the table."

"Or you. Maybe *you* stepped on the cover before *you* put it on the table."

"Yeah, whatever. Let's just finish this job."

I'm as far up as I can go, finally getting a chance to catch my breath. I look up and see wisps of clouds in a sky that goes on forever with layers of pink and orange.

Do you know why people look to the sky when they pray, Shah-jan? Do you know why we hang flags so far above our heads? Because we want to touch that sky, the sky that turns from blue to purple to pink and orange. You can find all colors in the sky. The sun, the moon, the stars, and the clouds—it has room for them all. That's why we love this country, my king. It is like the sky at our feet.

Here I am, as close to the sky as I can get, but feeling like there's no room for me in it.

"Where do I go from here, Mom?" I whisper. "I just want to go home. Why can't we just go home?"

A pigeon lands on the fire escape. He doesn't seem the least bit frightened of me and coos as he looks for the perfect perch on the metal railing. A moment later, a second pigeon joins him. Their voices are gentle, like wind chimes. They are not my pigeons, but they make me feel like I'm closer to home.

I know Auntie Seema's building is on this street, but I

don't know which one it is. It might even be on this block. I peek out and try to match these buildings up with the one I remember seeing on my mom's cell phone. The movers are still going in and out of the building. I see them struggle with a brown leather sofa. They're snapping at each other as they move forward and back a few times, trying for the right angle to fit this couch through the entrance.

"Turn to the left a little more. The left. The left, I said!"

"My left or your left?"

"My left!"

"So typical. It's always about you."

They disappear into the entrance with the sofa, their voices muffled by the walls. It's just me and the pigeons again.

The two of them coo at me together now. I look at them carefully, since I've trained myself to tell pigeons apart. One has gray feathers with two black stripes running across his back. The other is the same shade of gray but with darker, mottled feathers in the middle of his back and a shimmery purple area right around his neck. They both have fiery orange eyes with a central dark spot and reddish feet that look like lizard skin.

They look up and I follow their gaze. There are six or seven other pigeons on the rooftop, just a few feet over from where I'm crouched.

"Is this your home?" I whisper. It was the stories my

mom told me about pigeons in Afghanistan soaring miles through the sky but always returning home that pulled me to the roof of our building. I wondered why pigeons wouldn't just keep going if they were free to fly. What would keep them coming back? I learned that they come back because they learn to trust that home will be a place that treats them well, that feeds them, that will reunite them with their family and friends.

And I want, more than anything, to flap my wings and go back home to Elkton. That's where I belong.

That's when I spot four people coming down the block. I pull myself into a tight ball. Are my eyes playing tricks on me? I poke my head out by a hair. It's true. I see Liz and her mother walking down the sidewalk along with Officer Khan and a woman in baggy blue jeans and a dark-orange sweater. Her gold earrings catch the light and swing as she walks.

Auntie Seema! My heart jumps. How is this possible? I can hear them talking but can't make out the words until they are almost directly beneath me.

"Look, I think you and your daughter can go on home now. No need for you to walk around with us." That's Officer Khan's voice. He's caught his breath but still sounds frustrated.

"Fine, fine. But I just want to make sure you find him," Liz's mother insists.

"Mom, I don't think . . . ," Liz says, but I can't hear the rest of what she says. In a second, her mother cuts her off.

"Liz, *amor*, it's in the hands of the police now. We need to let them do their job."

There is more talking, and then I spy Liz and her mother walking down toward the end of the block and turning the corner. That leaves Auntie Seema and Officer Khan below me. I wish I could signal to Auntie Seema that I'm here, but Officer Khan has been after me since I left the hospital. I can't throw myself into his arms now.

"I don't know what else to do to help you," Auntie Seema says. Her voice makes me want to shout. I've been so desperate to find her, and she's only a few feet away from me.

"We'll find him soon. He's in the neighborhood, and he can't possibly run forever."

"I can't believe he's gotten all the way here. I never would have expected that."

I'm proud to hear her say that. I didn't think I'd get all the way here, either, but I had to try. And I did make it this far. It just might not be enough.

"Once we find him, we won't bother you for anything else. We appreciate all your cooperation so far. And you have my card. Please call me the second you see or hear from him."

"Of course, Officer!"

My stomach does a somersault. Auntie Seema's ready to turn me over. She's just promised to call Officer Khan the second she hears from me. I feel betrayed and a little dumb for not seeing this coming. Maybe I was mistaken to think Auntie Seema would be on my side and willing to look after me. It looks like I've gotten everything wrong.

"I'm going back to my apartment in case he turns up there," Auntie Seema says. Officer Khan mumbles some kind of reply that I cannot hear. I watch as Auntie Seema flings a multicolored scarf around her neck and lets it drape down her back. She walks with her hands in her pockets but her head is turning left to right. She's probably looking for me, wanting to turn her delinquent nephew in to the police.

Officer Khan gets back on his phone.

"Yup, yup. Got it. Be there in five." I see him take off too. The movers grunt and tell each other to move in one direction or the other. One of them wonders if the police officer is going to make them move the truck that's been taking up two parking spots in front of the apartment building.

With two beats of their charcoal wings, the pigeons float to the rooftop to join their friends. There they are, closer to the sky than I am. Actually, they're closer to the sky than I'll ever be. I don't think I've ever felt so alone.

I cover my head with my hands. I don't think I've ever

thought about giving up until this moment. Even thinking of how far I've come, into a city that terrified my mother, doesn't help me right now. Maybe, just maybe, I should walk down this fire escape and march myself over to Officer Khan. He didn't seem like such a bad guy after all. I think he is just trying to do his job. I should have done my job when my mother was taken away. I should have been her son, sticking with her no matter what.

I've made up my mind, I realize. I'm tired of feeling ashamed. I'm tired of running, especially since the person I've been running to has just said she'll turn me in. There's a small sense of relief in making this decision, even if it's the opposite of what I want.

The pigeons are cooing again, their heads wobbling about. I look back at the street when I hear another car approach. It's a police vehicle. I bet it's going to be Officer Khan but I can't see inside. After a couple of minutes, I hear the car door open. Ready to start the long climb down the stairs, I wait to see if it's Officer Khan. But the policeman who gets out of the car is not Officer Khan. It's someone I've never seen before, although he's wearing the same blue uniform. He scans the block up and down, then taps on the rear window of the car. He points at something in the distance and then walks away, leaving the car.

I know it's silly, but I don't want to turn myself in to anyone but Officer Khan. I started with him, and want to finish with him too. Maybe I won't have to answer as many questions. Maybe he will help me figure out how to send a message to my mom. There was a kindness in his eyes that I hope will still be there when I end this.

I see a shape move closer to the rear window of the police car. There is a person inside. I strain my eyes to see who it is. The person, as if sensing my interest, moves closer to the window. I see one hand and then another pressed against the glass. Then I see a face.

I nearly scream.

My mother is in the back of the police car.

My mother! I am on my feet. How quickly can I get down there?

The pigeons take off, gray wings against a rainbow sky.

I won't leave her this time.

I race down the fire escape as quickly as I can. I'm on the fourth story, then the third, then the second. I look at the police car. My mother's staring straight ahead, probably looking to see if the police officer is coming back for her.

I need to get to her first.

It's a long jump from here to the ground, but the movers still have furniture laid out between the truck and the building's entrance. There's a set of chairs, a wardrobe, and a mattress covered in plastic. I look down. I'm at least ten feet off the hard sidewalk, but this is no time to be afraid. I climb onto the railing of the fire escape, spread my arms out, and launch myself off like a pigeon going home.

I land on the mattress, the plastic crinkling beneath me. I tumble off onto the sidewalk and explode into the street, my hands on the door of the police car before my mother can figure out what's happening. I see her jump backward in the car until she sees my face.

"Shah!" she cries.

"Madar!" I shout. I'm pulling at the door from the outside, but it's locked. She pulls from the inside, with both hands, and can't get it open. I'm not surprised but I am disappointed. I was hoping for a break, just this once.

My heart is aching to see my mother in a locked police car.

"Shah-jan, you're okay! Where have you been? I was so worried!"

"Madar, we have to get out of here!" I'll answer her questions later. Right now, I've got to figure out a way to get her out of the police car. And I've got to make it quick, before the movers come back out for their next round and before the police officer comes back to his car.

"The police officer will be back," she shouts, her voice muffled by the glass of the car window.

"I know!" I'm trying not to shout because I don't want to draw attention. I glance down the street to see if anyone's coming our way. The coast is still clear. "I'll break the glass, Madar. I can hide us. I just need to get you out of the car!"

I pound on the glass with my fists, hating that I'm not strong enough to crack it.

"No! Shah-jan, no!" she cries frantically.

She still doesn't think I can handle this. I know she's scared but I've been scared too. That's the only thing that's kept me going from the gas station in Elkton to the train station to the hospital and into the tall city of Manhattan. I've been scared every step of the way, but I've been more scared of losing my mom forever, so I kept going.

"Shah! The police are—"

I look for something to use to break the car window. I see that the movers have left a dolly on the sidewalk, so I leap across the street and grab it. It's two pieces of wood on metal wheels, something used to move heavy boxes. It's the heaviest thing I see so it'll have to do. I pick it up and start to run toward the police car, the dolly raised high over my determined head.

"Shah! No! Don't do this!"

How else can we be together? I want to ask my mother. I'm lost without her. I'm sobbing and so is she.

"Move away from the window, Madar!" But she doesn't. She's shouting something that I can't hear over my sobs. That's why I'm hesitating. That's why I still have the dolly raised over my head, ready to crash it through the police car window, when I hear a voice boom down the street.

"Don't you dare, kid!"

It's the police officer who trapped my mom in the car. He's running toward me. I look at my mother and she's got her palms flat against the window, tears streaming down her cheeks. Her eyes look red and tired.

Officer Khan comes charging around the corner. His elbows pumping, he is running faster than any of the marathon runners I saw today.

"Jason D!" he yells.

I look at my mother and let the dolly fall to the ground. I let them come to me, never taking my eyes off my mother. Maybe we won't be able to run. That's okay. The important thing is that I'm not leaving her. I'll fight with everything I have to stay with my mother.

And now I know how hard I can fight.

Thirty-Two

Officer Khan grabs me by the shoulders. He doesn't need to, though. I'm done running. I stand there, his hands holding me up, as the other officer unlocks the police car.

"I'm so sorry. We always keep the doors locked from the inside and I . . ."

My mom bolts out of the car before he can finish explaining. I'm in her arms, feeling like a million pounds have been lifted off my shoulders.

"Madar!" I want to say so much more, but it's just not coming out right now.

Officer Khan is on his phone.

"We're here with him," he says. He's got one hand on

his hip and his eyes glued to me as if I might take off again. "No obvious injuries. Seems to be all right. Yeah, call off the Amber Alert."

My mother's fingers are pressing into my arms, but I'm glad for it. I can feel her heartbeat, and have my arms wrapped around her waist. We're leaning against the police car. The movers have come back out of the building and are looking at us with curiosity.

"You're not in Afghanistan," I say to my mother.

"No, *jan-em*. I'm right here."

"But I saw them take you."

"Is that why you ran?" my mother asks me, her voice trembling. I nod. I've replayed that morning in my head over and over again. I don't think I'll ever forget it.

"I was at the gas station and I saw them. I saw you in that car, leaving."

"My sweet boy, I'm so sorry. I never wanted you to be so scared!"

"I'll go with you, Madar. I'll go with you to Afghanistan. I don't care if it's dangerous. I don't want to be here alone."

"We're not going anywhere, *jan-em*. We have a lot to figure out, but I think we'll be okay."

"What do you mean?"

My mother looks at the police officers. She takes a deep breath and starts to explain.

"I am asking for permission to stay. When I told them how I came here and all about your father and why I was too afraid to go back, they told me I should apply for asylum. There are many papers to fill out and I will have to tell my story, but I have faith and hope. I think we will be okay, Shah-*jan-em*."

When she calls me her king, I think maybe it's possible that we will be okay. I'm so relieved.

"I want to be home with you, Madar-jan."

My mother kisses my forehead and runs her fingers through my hair.

"You are my home," my mother says. Her voice is as sweet as honey to me.

Officer Khan puts a hand on my shoulder again.

"I think we should get you back to the hospital for a checkup. You look okay, but we want to be on the safe side."

"I'm fine. I don't need to go to the hospital."

"Jason D, you had a pretty bad head trauma. You were supposed to be recovering, taking it easy. I don't think that's what you've been doing today. I'm still pretty baffled. I mean, one minute you were at the hospital. Next thing I know you and your friend have vanished, then you take off on a police horse, and then you're wandering around West Seventy-Fourth Street. Did I miss anything?"

No, I haven't exactly taken it easy today. And I'm proud of that.

"The Central Park Zoo," I say matter-of-factly.

"You went to the zoo? Whoa. Max didn't mention that."

I stand straight up.

"You talked to Max?"

Officer Khan nods, a small smile on his face.

"She's fine. She's a tough cookie, just like you."

"Yeah," I say, thinking of the steely look Max gets in her eyes when she's made up her mind about something. "She's more than a cookie."

Officer Khan nods again slowly and puts his hands up in some form of apology. "I stand corrected," he says cheerfully. His phone rings and he turns away from us to answer it. The other police officer steps in.

"The hospital is a good idea. Better to be on the safe side, as my friend here said."

My arms wrap around my mother again. My lips press tight. "I'm not going anywhere without her."

"We wouldn't expect you to," the officer says. I finally feel like I can breathe.

We hear the rattling of a truck door, and I see the movers are back out by the curb, their yellow shirts dark with sweat stains around the armpits and down the middle of their backs.

"Where'd you put the dolly, Charlie?" the taller one asks, saying Charlie in a way that makes it almost rhyme with *dolly*.

"My name isn't Charlie," mutters his partner.

"Could have been worse. I could've called you Polly."

"You know what? Sometimes you're a real . . ."

"Hey, there it is! What are you guys doing with our dolly?"

The dolly, of course, is at my feet. It is upside down, wheels sticking up into the air and still spinning, like a beetle stuck on its back.

"That's the kid you were looking for?" the taller mover calls out cheerfully. "You found him!"

"Where was he?" shouts the one *not* named Charlie.

"We're all set here, thanks, fellas." Officer Khan shuts down their questions. He puts the dolly back on its wheels and kicks it across the street. Not-Charlie picks it up just as his friend looks at the mattress and the clear plastic cover marked with my footprints.

"Hey, Polly," he says, scratching his head. "Didn't your mother ever warn you about monkeys jumping on the bed?"

Thirty-Three

I am in the back of the police car, squeezed in between my mom and Auntie Seema. They're staring at me with weird looks on their faces. I almost wonder if I've sprouted a second head or some other curiosity.

"Shah. Really," Auntie Seema says, her voice chiding me gently. "You really think I want to put you in jail? Ah. This many years and this is what your son thinks, Rona?"

"I'm sorry, Auntie Seema. It's just that I heard you talking to . . ." I let my voice drop off because Officer Khan is driving the police car we're in, and I still feel bad about lying to him and running off when he was only trying to help.

"Oh, I'm just glad you're all right. And I'm glad you

were coming to me. That makes me very happy. You know I would do *anything* for you." She squeezes me against her. She smells like she always does, a mix of incense and the special kind of dark tea she drinks. I can see flecks of different colors underneath her nailbeds and on her cuticles. Her patterned scarf hangs loosely around her neck, and her eyes are soft and brown. I do feel a lot better with her here.

"I've been telling your mother for years to apply for asylum. Who could turn her away after all your father did and what happened to him? And after all he did for those soldiers?"

"I was afraid, Seema."

My mother looks like she needs to hear something. I want to take away that feeling she has right now. "I know what it's like to be afraid, Mom. But I think we're going to be okay."

I haven't said much, but something in my mother seems to relax. Auntie Seema reaches over and puts a hand over my mother's.

I'm brought back to the hospital I left. It's not the closest hospital, but it's the one where they did all those tests on me, and they don't want me to have to do it all over again somewhere new. They check me in to the same emergency room. A nurse and a doctor look me over from head to toe. The doctor, a man old enough to be someone's grand-father, reads my information in the computer system and pokes at the bump on my head. He shines a light in my eyes and makes me balance on one foot. He asks me a lot of questions about what I did once I left the hospital.

He shakes his head, not in disappointment but in a sort of admiration.

"I've been doing this a long time, kid. A really long time. And I've never seen anyone manage a grand escape."

I sit up a little straighter, as if he's patted me on the back. I wasn't expecting him to say that, especially since this is the hospital I ran away from.

"But let me ask you something. Just out of curiosity," he says, his hands in the pockets of his white coat.

My mother and Auntie Seema are sitting in visitor chairs inside the room. They lean in, anxious to hear every bit of this conversation. They've been suspicious, too, that I've left out some really dangerous part of the story. I think if I told them I wrestled a tiger in the middle of Times Square they would believe me right now.

"Sure," I say. "What is it?"

"How'd you get off the unit upstairs? We keep some pretty tight security up there for the kids."

"Oh, that." I smile to myself, thinking of how Max swiped Nurse Eric's badge and the way we soaped the alarm bracelets off our wrists. I could tell him about it, but that would give away too much. I'm no longer Manhattan Doe here, but I can still be a bit of a mystery. "I can't tell you that part, but if you're ever trapped somewhere, feel free to give me a call."

The doctor's eyebrows spring upward and he lets out a good belly laugh. My mother puts a hand to the side of her face, half-embarrassed and half-amused by my response. Auntie Seema claps her hands together happily because she's okay with breaking rules sometimes.

I watch him walk out of the room and see Officer Khan standing in the hallway beside a tall counter. He's filling out some forms. I get off the exam table, putting a second hospital gown over the one I'm wearing to cover my backside. I need to look proper for what I'm about to do.

Auntie Seema and my mom are on their feet right away.

"I want to talk to Officer Khan for a second," I explain, seeing the concern on their faces. Auntie Seema puts a hand on my mom's elbow. They both sit back down, and I walk over to the door. I poke my head out and clear my throat to catch Officer Khan's attention. When he looks my way, I step out of the room and into the hallway, closing the door behind me.

"I just want to say that I'm really sorry for not telling you the truth," I say slowly. "I know you were trying to help me."

Officer Khan puts the papers down on the counter.

"I don't like what you did, Jason D, but I get why you did it. And I wish you'd never felt like people in uniforms were the bad guys. That's not what we are. I hope you'll see that now."

"I do," I say. I feel my face flush suddenly with embarrassment. "And I didn't think you were the bad guy. I thought I was. I mean, it's my mom who broke the rules."

Officer Khan presses his lips together and looks at me for a long moment. Then he walks over to me and looks me straight in the eye in a way most grown-ups don't.

"You are not a bad guy. Your mom is not a bad guy. Sometimes people break rules because they think it's the best thing they can do. Sometimes it is the right thing to do. Sometimes it's not. These are tough questions, and tough questions never have easy answers. But don't blame your mom. She did what she did because she was scared. You know her better than anyone else. Listen to what your heart thinks about her, not any piece of paper."

I stare at the cold tiles of the hospital floor. It's true. I've been ashamed that my mother hid so much from me and broke the rules. When people on television talk about walls and documents, I never thought they were talking about my mom. But I know Officer Khan is right. My mother has never wanted to be on the wrong side of any rule. She's a good person with bad options.

"Thanks," I say. He seems to get what I mean by that

one small word. And the look on his face makes me feel bold enough to make a big ask.

"I wanted to ask for your help with something." This is one of the reasons I didn't put up much of a fight when Officer Khan told me I'd have to go back to the hospital for a checkup.

"What is it, buddy?" Officer Khan asks me.

"I want to see Max."

"Ah," he says. "I bet you do."

I've been thinking about Max since I left her on the sidewalk. I've been hoping she hasn't gotten into too much trouble and that she's not too sick. Running away from the hospital was harder on her than it was on me. But I get why she did it. She's a good person who wanted a chance to make a choice for herself.

"Let me give her parents a call and see what they say. Maybe you can return her backpack to her."

"The backpack I left on the sidewalk?"

Officer Khan gives me a playful nudge.

"It's my job to collect evidence from the scene of the crime, and I store that evidence in the safety of my trunk."

I think of the phone and the notebook, the message I wrote for my new friend, the messages she wrote for herself. I think of the brochure about Vincent van Gogh and the incredible art that came from his brain. I want her to have that bag back.

Things start moving. Officer Khan talks to my doctor. The doctor calls a nurse upstairs. Next thing I know, I have the backpack on my shoulders like I did for so much of today, and I'm in the elevator again, headed to the pediatric floor for the second time in three days.

Max is in the same room. She's sitting on her bed, watching her feet dangle off the side. She looks a little tired but otherwise okay. She turns to the door when she hears the knock. I'm happy to see her face brighten when she spots me.

"Jason D!" she exclaims. She jumps off the bed and squeezes me tight. Her parents are standing by the wall, holding hands and looking like they might cry. Max and I sure have turned all the adults into emotional wrecks. "You did it!"

My face breaks into a wide grin.

"I heard you found your aunt! I knew you would make it."

"I guess I did."

I open my mouth to say more—to tell her that I couldn't have done it without her help and that I wished she could have been there with me for the whole day and about how I managed to sneak onto a food truck and away from Officer Khan when he was just a block away. But then I shut my mouth, because I don't think it would be a good idea to boast about the things we've done just yet in front of my mom, Auntie Seema, and Max's parents.

Instead, I hand her the teal backpack that kept me company when she was gone.

Our families are busy shaking hands and apologizing to one another for our behavior. That seems a little silly to me, but sometimes adults just can't stand saying nothing.

"I dropped your bag, but the police officer picked it up. I wanted to give it back to you. Your phone's in there."

"I tried calling you on that phone but you never answered."

"That was you?" I remember staring at the incoming calls, wondering if I should answer.

"When I got to the hospital, they told me your mom was looking for you. I tried to tell you, but you didn't pick up."

I want to kick myself.

"Yup," she says, taking the bag from me. She looks over at the cluster of adults in the corner. They're talking to one another while stealing glances at us from the corners of their eyes.

"My surgery is tomorrow," Max says quietly. She's toying with the zipper of her bag as she says this, her eyelashes fluttering nervously.

I search for the right words. Why is it so hard to figure out what to say?

"You're going to be fine, Max. I bet you don't have

anything to worry about, and I'm going to come visit you when it's over and you're back to your regular self so I can tell you I told you so."

Max looks up sharply. She didn't miss what I said. And I do believe it. I don't think anything could change Max, not even surgery on her brain. I think she'll always be Max, and I'll always want to be her friend.

"And I bet you're going to be famous now," she tells me with her head tilted and her mouth in a smart twist. "You're the kid who ran up and down Manhattan and escaped the cops. Don't let all this celebrity stuff go to your head, all right? You're a long way from Hollywood."

Max is still grinning when we leave her hospital room. She follows me into the hallway, looking small but strong in her hospital gown and with a fresh hospital security bracelet on her wrist.

"By the way," I say cooly over my shoulder, "you might want to check out the pictures on your phone. I'm closer to Hollywood than you think."

Thirty-Four

*I*t's a Friday in December and my mother is frantically chopping tomatoes, cucumbers, and cilantro. The rice, the beef stew, and the fried eggplant are all simmering in the oven. Auntie Seema is setting our small table and shaking her head to see my mother so anxious.

"You've never made such a fuss for me coming over," she says, acting as if her feelings are really hurt.

"That's not true, Seema," my mother mumbles, and Auntie Seema laughs because my mother's right. She cooks for two full days any time Auntie Seema comes to visit.

It's not until the doorbell buzzes that I realize I'm as anxious as my mother. I've cleaned the bedroom we share about twenty times and straightened the pillows on the couch so many times they look scared to move.

"I'll get it!" I shout.

"Shah-jan, don't run," my mom calls out, though she's practically hopping to put away the chopping board and the strainer, that metal sky full of stars. "Remember Ms. Raz!"

Ms. Raz. When I got back, my mother sat down and told Ms. Raz everything. The police had come by the building the day I ran off and asked her lots of questions. It turns out Ms. Raz was really worried about me. She went out looking for me in the neighborhood and wrestled my backpack away from that little angry dog. She told my mother, when she brought the backpack to our door, that she's not just our landlord, she's also our neighbor and friend. She didn't say it with a smile on her face or any mushy hugs. But she said it, and she meant it.

My father's pictures were still in perfect condition despite being under those little paws. Now those photographs are on the side table in our living room. I spent a lot of time staring at them before I slid them back into the frames. I think I do actually look like him. My nose has the same slope. My eyebrows are just as dark. Maybe I'll be a story-telling journalist, too, one day. I think of all the good things my mother told me about Afghanistan, and I think I see a little bit of that in me.

Maybe I should start with telling the story of an

Afghan-American boy who traveled to the end of the earth for his family, riding a stallion and relying on the friendship and hospitality of people who were fellow countrymen but also strangers. It kind of sounds like an Afghan story. It also sounds like an American story. I guess I don't have to choose—like Liz said, it can be both.

"Seema, you are sure my clothes are good?"

Auntie Seema has a glass of mango juice in one hand. She looks at my mother's freshly ironed black slacks and sky-blue blouse. Her lapis lazuli pendant dangles from her neck. Auntie Seema points to her own jeans, ripped at the knees, and her red flannel shirt.

"Almost as good as mine," she says, and slips onto the couch. She can spend weeks arranging spots of color on a canvas or re-creating a desert scene. She cares about us. She cares about making sure every scrap of paper goes into a blue recycling bin. Nothing else seems to matter much. I like that about her.

I throw the door open.

"Hey, Jason D," Max says. Her cheeks are flushed from the walk up three flights of stairs. She looks good, like she's woken up from the best night's sleep and an awesome dream. Her parents are standing behind her, looking a bit shy.

"Hope we're not too early. We were anxious to have our first authentic Afghan dinner!"

It's really good to see her. There's so much to tell her, so much to ask her. Does she remember every little thing about being Max? What about our day together? Does she remember the rat that poked its head out in the alley and the look on Dr. Shabani's face when we saw her in the marathon? Has she been back to her tree circle since her surgery? I want to tell her so much. I want to tell her about the lawyer who helped write my mother's story, filling page after page with the hard truth behind the things she did. I want to tell her about the letter we got that says my mother might get real permission to stay in the country and officially become an American, like me. I wonder if I can take her to the roof and show her my pigeons and the amazing view of Elkton, my hometown. I wonder if we'll have enough time tonight to get to all of it. We might not. We might just have to start small.

"Hey, Max," I say with a laugh, remembering my manners and Afghan hospitality. I move aside and point an arm into our apartment. "Welcome to our home."

Author's Note

I am not Jason D but I can surely relate to him. My parents came to the United States just a few years before I was born. Many family members, fleeing a war-torn Afghanistan, followed in their footsteps or fled to other countries as refugees. I don't know how old I was when I started learning words like *affidavits*, *documents*, *visas*, *asylum*, and *amnesty*. They are the necessary vocabulary of an immigrant family, especially one hailing from a war-ravaged nation.

My parents had visions of a brighter future in America and they found the land of opportunity, freedom, and liberty they'd heard about a half world away. My parents each have photos from their early days in the country with Lady Liberty standing tall just behind them, a beacon to those "huddled masses yearning to breathe free."

In more recent years, immigration has become a deeply polarizing issue. Who should have the privilege of living in the United States? What responsibility does this country have to help families escaping danger around the world? There are no simple answers to these tough questions, but we can talk about them with decency and compassion, always remembering that we are talking about human beings. We're all branches of the same tree, the Sufi poet Hafiz wrote in a gorgeous verse that hangs in my living room.

The relationship between Afghanistan and the United States is a long and storied one. In recent years, many Afghans have worked as translators for the US military stationed in Afghanistan. They do so at great risk, as many have been accused of treason or spying. Many have had their lives threatened. Far too many have been killed. So many Americans have stood up in support of those interpreters who were promised opportunities to come to the United States. And countless immigrants begin growing their American patriotism well before they reach this nation. I hope Jason D's story will help readers understand why immigration is complex and important.

And then we have Max. Max is dealing with a very different struggle, but one that also has her questioning her identity. She is a girl with seizures, but she is so much more than that. Naturally, her parents worry about her, but she refuses to let any diagnosis stop her from plunging into the very enchanting New York City.

As a pediatrician, I've had the privilege of watching children soar despite diagnoses. Diabetes, cancer, seizures—these aren't identities. Children know that and valiantly live their lives to the fullest. They are superheroes, with or without the capes flapping behind their shoulders.

To all the superheroes holding this story in your very capable hands, this world will test you in big or small ways. Maybe it already has. Know that nothing defines you but your heart and your actions. When the time comes, go ahead and let those superpowers dazzle the world.

Acknowledgments

Zoran, Zayla, Kyrus, and Cyra—thank you for the daily bouquets of chaos, encouragement, love, laughter, and the questions that halt me in my tracks. Along with Boba and Yaya, you all make it impossible and important for me to write these stories. Amin, thank you for always having my best interests at heart, for being my sounding board, and for dreaming bigger than life. Thank you to my astute agent, Sarah Heller, for nudging this story in the right direction. Grateful hugs to my editor, Rosemary Brosnan, for your principled guidance, for encouraging me to tackle the hard issues, and for believing in young readers. Much of this story stems from my experiences working with children like Max. To the young rock stars in my life— Nyla, Kylie, Arria, Mila, Sorab, Sarah, Henna—you all inspire me to write about incredible kids, and you might have even given me some material. My thanks to the many compassionate and skilled physicians who helped train me and to the teams of allied health professionals I've partnered with along the way. And, of course, a world of thanks to the children I've cared for and to their families for teaching me about bravery, grace, and illness.

Great books by
NADIA HASHIMI!

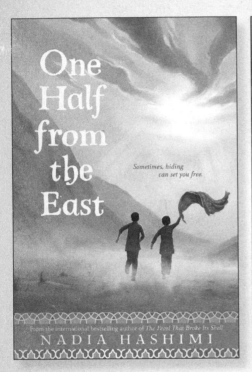

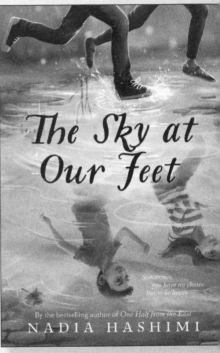

31901062465226